I0623650

COLD SNAP

Yuki Shirogane and the Winter Diamond Chronicles

Written by: Macky Santiago
Created by: Kahlil Santiago and Macky Santiago

BlueRoom Projects

BlueRoom
Projects

Copyright © 2020 Mark Santiago

All rights reserved

No part of this book may be reproduced, or stored in a retrieval system,
or transmitted in any form or by any means, electronic, mechanical,
photocopying, recording, or otherwise, without express written permission
of the publisher.

Cover design and Illustraion by: Kahlil Santiago

ISBN: 978-1-952995-03-3

Firstly, I dedicate this book to Kahlil Santiago. Pretty sure you'll never forget that era when we were kids up in that attic, when standard operating procedure was for me to yap away telling stories while you drew out characters next to a small mountain of colored markers. This thing here that we did has the same energy.

Finally, I dedicate this book to Alexa, who (with Kahl in the actual Blue Room) dreamed that we three would be able to tell the stories I had in my head together. Not just out loud with said yapping, but with the 'written word'.

I love you both dearly.

CONTENTS

DRAMATIS PERSONAE

The Galactic Defense Force Conglomerate and its Vassal Worlds

o   **Captain Nandru Zavus** – Most decorated captain of the Conglomerate. Alliance double agent.

o   **Queen Octavia V** – Supreme ruler of the United Worlds

o   **Princess Lahani Mardress** – Heir to the throne of the planet Faldan (currently under Conglomerate sanction)

o   **Princess Kelna Mardress** – Second in line to the throne of Faldan

The Crew of the Sol Pernix

o   **Theron Jaeger** – Captain of the Sol Pernix. Notorious galactic mercenary and smuggler.

o   **Tala Mienstrom** – First mate of the Sol Pernix. Sniper.

o   **Walsher Jaeger** – Pilot

o   **Summer Bennet** – Medic

o   **Charles Bennet** – Weapons and demolition

o   **Dropshot** – Synthoid hacker and engineer

Highly Encrypted Transmission
Origin: Decomissioned Conglomerate Space Relay

The cubs are in the den and the den is impenetrable. Package must be secured before the parliament lands. Sprint, not marathon. They can smell even the smallest of weaves and have been trained to hunt for snow. No charms on day zero until further notice.

Highly Encrypted Transmission
Origin: Vector 772

Copy. Dress warm. Cold snap imminent.

Field Captain Yuki Shirogane's Log
Location: Winter Diamond, Vector 772

Just want to state for the record that even if they didn't assign me to this op, I would have found some way to help. But everyone on the council knows my operative team is the only one in the entire Triune Alliance that has both the best chance of success and the lowest potential casualty rate.

I take offense at the last part on behalf of my non-organic crew. I so wanted to correct them and say our casualty rate is low because we're pretty damn hard to kill, not because I'm the only organic life form on the team.

But I held my tongue at the briefing. I won't let them get away with that though. Not forever. My crew deserves better. Sure, they're the most powerful elite assault robots in the known galaxies. But they have feelings too, you know?

Note to self. Send a formal complaint to Admiral Stormcrow to make it clear that I don't quite care for the council's tone about my crew. Especially not when we're their best bet at taking on the Conglomerate, and certainly not when we're their best chance at pulling off this mission.

And we're ever so efficient. I even made a to do list!

- ~~Refuel the Anargian core fusion cells~~

- ~~Buy fifteen Jandrium tubes for the baby-bots~~

- ~~Finally get that life support system alarm fixed~~

- ~~Restock ammunition for front and rear cannons~~

- Get a full body rejuvenation treatment

- Rescue Faldanian princesses from heavily armed space station exercising despotic control over their home planet before they are taken away to a Conglomerate black site, without being identified or killed

CHAPTER ONE

I should have started with the rejuve treatment.

But instead, I'm here. Cloaked and successfully hoodwinking both the Faldan planetary defense rig and the Conglomerate Class Sensor array of the Faldan Space Station.

As far as anyone in this solar system is concerned, we don't exist right now. They don't have to know we're nearby. Nor is it any of their business that we're snug and comfy on the bridge of one of the known galaxy's prettiest ships.

Well, most of us anyway.

"Forty-five seconds to target deployment site." Bellona warbles happily through my earpiece. Hooked up to the Diamond's sensor array, she's quite literally more in the ship than "on" it.

"Aye, good on you, Bellona. Cheery in the face of imminent death. Been campaigning for years for that to be our slogan." Doctor Capaldi responds, hovering quietly next to me. "Alliance Operative Team Designation: Cold Snap. Cheery in the face of imminent death."

"Mission now, sarcasm later, Doctor." I say lovingly. "Jean Philippe, you've been out there a while. Sit rep."

"Even with your revised cloaking tech, I can only redirect attention from us for so long without their sensors picking us up."

Bellona adds.

"But Bellona, *mon ange*, with your skills we are more than safe, yes? Practically invincible! Practically unstoppable!" Jean Philippe interjects. "Practically..."

"Practically time you finished hacking the entry point open? Not that I don't love the sound of your voice, JP." I teased. He hates it when I call him that.

"The reprimand, the flattery and the slight. Mademoiselle Capitaine has learned her lessons in subtle manipulation well. After all, her teacher is anything but less than excellent." Jean Philippe's tone is more playful and soothing. Which tells me something isn't right.

"Come on, Jean Philippe. Report." I ask. "We only have..."

"Ten seconds to deployment site." Bellona warns. Cheery still, but I can sense the edge to it, not just in her voice, but also along our connection in the neuroweave.

There are days the neuroweave feels like a curse, since I can hear and feel everyone all at once. Makes travelling across the galaxy in a ship extra crowded because they're in my head too. But on missions —and especially ops like this one — I wouldn't trade it for the universe.

I always hate admitting it, but Queen Octavia really is a genius. Evil. But a genius. I'm just thrilled that we can use all that tech she put in us against her in situations like the one we're in now. Though currently, the crew and I are more anxious than thrilled.

My heart pounds as the ship annexes itself to the side of the space station's underbelly. We chose one of the non-functional

refinery exhaust ports as a point of entry, mostly because nobody in their right mind would ever want to attempt entry
through here.

"E... *voila*! Open sesame." Jean Philippe exclaims, followed by
silence. Too much silence.

"Talk to me, Jean Philippe." I ask.

"*Alor*... it seems none of the codes work." He responded.

"You mean all seven hundred docking and entry codes I paid
fifty-three thousand credits for are duds." I say. If I ever get my
hands on that weasel of a code broker Breacher Kane, I'm going
to make him eat that ugly hat and shoot him in his one functioning kneecap.

"I have my own protocols..." Jean Philippe offered, but Bellona
cut him off.

"The Conglomerate knows our unique neuroweave signatures,
Jean Philippe." Bellona says, strain cutting through her cheery
tone. "And we have... Oh goodness, one minute and fifty-four
seconds until the next security sweep eliminates the last of our
cloaking protocols. We'll be on her Magic Mirror for sure."

The Magic Mirror is the Queen's nasty new "toy" that detects
and breaks down cloaking technology. It uses frequencies and
counter frequencies that ultimately nullify cloaks or overwhelm the tech powering them. It can also track, scan, and
triangulate the location of anything within its scope of deployment.

Evil despots shouldn't also be mad geniuses, or vice versa. And
yet, here we are. a little closer to death because of it.

We'd been successful so far at evading her, thanks to whatever countermeasures Jean Philippe and the crew rigged up. I paid through the nose to buy enough unique cloaking protocols to make it work. It's bought us some time.

Since warping into the planet's orbit and force docking onto the underbelly of the station, we'd burnt through thirty-six unique cloaking protocols. Thirty-seven will be the magic number for this mission... mostly because we're down to our last one.

"I am aware that the Conglomerate systems know us intimately and wish us ill, like a badly jilted lover. But am I not the best saboteur in the galaxy?" Jean Philippe says. He's charming, but he never brags without reason. He has something. I can feel it. And the others can too.

"Whatever it is, do it. Or we're toast in...?" I ask Bellona.

"One minute, thirty-two seconds." She offers.

"I will need two minutes to get past their decryption unidentified." Jean Philippe says. "And yes, we do not have the luxury of time, but I have been studying *Le Miroir Magique* since the Drallian incident. Since then, I have devised a prototype scrambler that, once mounted physically onto any of the mirror transponders, *should* buy us three full minutes of cloaking. All of us. Our energy signatures. Our neuroweave signatures. Operative word: *should*."

"Nearest transponder is two minutes away." Bellona adds, ever helpful. "Which is twice the actual time we have."

"I have devised the scrambler so it can be deployed at high velocity from far distances with no harm to the device itself." Jean Philippe says smugly. Even as he said the words high velocity, I could feel Mila move to exit the Diamond.

"Mila, you're up. Get the scrambler from Jean Philippe and fire it at the transponder. JP, I could kiss you." I smile.

"Alas, I have no lips and respond poorly to the shortening of my name, but I will accept accolades and credits." He says.

"In position. Target is three thousand yards away." Mila says. That's an easy mark for a targeting bot of her caliber, since all of us were made to be the elite of the galaxy's elite.

"Thirty Seconds!" Bellona announces.

"Take the shot, Mila." I say.

"The transponder is shielded. Will have to disrupt the shield to give me an opening." Mila says.

"Jean Philippe, time to share your toys." My heart hammers. We need to work together to pull this off. "Activate Link Tag Protocol. Let's play."

I plunge into the neuroweave and feel its familiar gravity. Every synapse in my brain fires in rapid, concurrent explosions until I am perfectly synchronized with Jean Philippe and Mila. Borrowing from Jean Philippe's programming, I lend the protocols for the shield scrambling tech to Mila as she prepares to fire on her first target.

This deep into the neuroweave, I sense everything through their systems.

Jean Philippe codes new protocols on the spot. It's like he's creating thread, then weaving it into cloth and shaping into a disguise... all while trying to crack the station's surface code.

I also sense Mila as she downloads the new skills and information she needs to use Jean Philippe's device. From there she'll analyze the natural fluctuation of the Magic Mirror's transponder shield energy signature and time the shot at just the right moment in the power cycle.

She'll disrupt the shield and deploy the scrambler. If the Conglomerate systems pick up a two or three second hitch, it can easily be dismissed as a routine surge.

"Twenty seconds until cloak failure!" Bellona informs us.

Meanwhile, Mila and I are still using Jean Philippe's protocols to analyze the shield's power cycles.

Seconds feel like hours until a pattern finally emerges.

"Analysis complete. Eight seconds until next power surge." Mila says.

"Cloak failure in ten. Nine. Eight..." Bellona counts down.

"Two seconds to make two shots. Could be worse." Doctor Capaldi says before I can stop him.

I am not superstitious by nature, but sometimes, you just do not want to tempt any higher powers. Of course, the reality is that, apart from the impossible, testing the higher powers is the other thing we do all the time.

Even before Bellona announces it, I feel it through her sensors.

"Sentry bots. Three of them. Seven meters and closing! Five seconds to cloak failure!" Bellona shouts, no mirth left in her voice, only urgency.

In a pure rush of adrenaline, I push past my first threshold of control and extend my consciousness to encompass all seven of my crew.

This is full interface.

This is the thing that makes me and my team arguably the most lethal force in the known galaxies: that all our minds can become one.

My mind is a field of explosions. A nebula of stars being birthed. No human mind has the capacity to interface with a machine in full, let alone an elite robot. But mine can. And not just with one machine, but with seven.

I was built this way. My home world and whatever else that could have belonged to me, were ripped away before I could even take my first breath. All so I could be forged into something that could do what I am doing now.

Everything it takes to achieve full interface with my crew happens in a flash. But time stretches when I'm submerged this deep into the neuroweave, and especially if I am interfaced with this many synthetic minds.

As our connection locks our minds in place, I don't even need to give commands as the remaining crew aboard the Diamond bursts into action.

I feel Iñigo and Leon launch out from the ship as Mick interfaces with the Diamond's cannons. Leon will be Iñigo's shield as he takes out the sentries, while Jean Philippe works with Bellona and scrambles the sentries' communications protocols. We need them to keep transmitting an all clear signal, and we need that signal to transmit on loop or this op is over.

In graceful half-times, I watch as Jean Philippe overclocks his processors with Bellona's help. He hacks both the ship and the sentries. His processors kick into overdrive as he duplicates the communication signal the sentry bots use, while finishing up the code that will "disguise" us before all Conglomerate tech on the station.

Iñigo's lumenblades slice through the first sentry, triggering a counterattack from the other two.

Bellona masks the weapons being discharged by weaving an "all clear" declaration into the false signal Jean Philippe beams back on behalf of the sentries. Nearby, Leon's deflector fields keep enemy fire from touching Iñigo.

At the eight second mark, Mila fires the shield scrambler. In a split second, she deploys Jean Philippe's new device.

Bellona's countdown reaches zero on the screen just as Iñigo slices the last sentry in half. For a few more seconds, nothing happens. Everything is bright, and I am in eight places at once, perceiving the universe in eight different ways.

Doctor Capaldi breaks my reverie and gathers my consciousness back to one singular point. It feels like having him help me up to my feet after laying still for a very long time or letting him guide me to a comfortable chair after hours of standing.

The universe dims, and I am once again looking at the control screen of the Diamond. I'm no longer in space surrounded by wrecked sentry bots. I am not docked on the space station or hooked up to its circuitry. I am not on the Diamond's hull taking aim at a target three thousand yards away.

I am Yuki again. And the Doctor, if he had lips, would have been smiling at me.

"Ye've done well, child. I'll patch Iñigo up and see what I can do about our new sentry bot friends. Should be able use them somehow when we infiltrate this new mess ye've gotten us into." He says, hovering beside me.

Gingerly, I place my hand on his head and smile. "Thank you, Doctor. Just try not to jinx us again. Bellona, sit rep?"

The Doctor leaves, grumbling about statistics and superstition as Bellona reports. "Minor injuries to Iñigo and Leon, Doctor Capaldi en route for patch up and retrieval. Mila opted to stand watch with Jean Philippe as he begins the revised hack. He only needs one minute out of the three he has bought us. Mick has disengaged and is heading to the bridge."

"Thank you, Bellona. Jean Philippe, time to infiltration?" I ask.

"Twenty seconds and counting." He says gleefully.

True enough, in exactly the promised amount of time, the exhaust port opens, and I guide my ship in.

The Winter Diamond docks inside the abandoned refinery and powers down. I stand and stretch, limbering up for the rescue mission to come. At full strength, I can manage a full interface with the whole crew about three times.

But with all the prep and finagling that had gone into this op, I've basically been running on no sleep for a week or two. And that means I most likely have only one full interface with all seven of them left for the day.

Really wish I had gone for that full body treatment now.

MACKY SANTIAGO

Encrypted Transmission
Origin: Alliance Capital Ship Haven Five,
Vector 559283

Yuki, I more than anyone, am loathe to send you on this mission. For years, I have endured questions about my bias towards you, and so, my sanctioning this retrieval op has been a surprise to the Alliance (myself included).

Let us hope our enemies will be equally surprised that we sent our most valuable asset directly behind their lines.

Our last encounter was not our best, so I just wanted to say that you have proven your point many times over.

Yes, you are no longer a child. Yes, you are easily one of the best, if not *the* best operative in the field.

Of course, I have not forgotten that "the blade unsheathed at the opportune time can fell both men and empires". I taught you this when we first found you, as you may recall.

I do confess that those days feel like lifetimes ago.

Our enemies deemed you and your crew defective. But I believe in the higher powers. Whatever hands of destiny wove you and your crew to gether (quite literally at that!) are weaving now still.

They thought you would be as harmless and inconsequential as snow fall. Instead, they will see you for the blade that you truly are.

Faldan will revolt if they know the princesses are safe. Whomever commands Faldan determines the course of this war. The highest probability of success is with you and your crew, whether I like it or not.

And I certainly do not.

The implications of what is to become of the girls after the Conglomerate takes them away is distressing. That Agent Zero has prom ised no help — nor can he be of help is even more so.

Your narrow window of success shrinks exponentially should the Conglomerate delegation arrive before you extract the targets. These odds are personally distressing to me.

It pains me to say we cannot risk any of our fleet to aid you, thanks to that blasted mirror! They'll know we're in the solar system the mo ment we exit warp space.

You won't be completely out of help though. If we can scrounge up enough funds, you just might get 'the best help money can buy'.

Don't pout. He's the best that we have on retainer and he's even given you a run for your money. Just be thankful he's on our side and that (I hope) our scandalously expensive tab he keeps harping on is more for bluster than it is for real.

Bring the girls home, Yuki. Bring every one of your crew home personally. That's an order.

      Mother

Encrypted Transmission
Origin: Vector 72930

Getting sentimental in your old age, Mother Ryn.

Just so you know, I'm pouting right now. In fact, I plan to pout for the entire mission. The princesses will see me, and they will call me Captain Pouty Face, and it will be all your fault.

I never asked for help. I have enough of a bone to pick with the Conglomerate to fuel this mission solely on a personal grudge.

Driven by justice. Fueled by spite.

Huh.

Remind me to engrave that on the Diamond.

And copy, Mother. I'll bring them home. All of them. And if Mr. Fancypants gets in my way, I'll feed him to Octavia myself.

CHAPTER TWO

It took Jean Philippe an hour to fully integrate himself into the Faldan Space Station systems. Not his finest moment, but it did give Doctor Capaldi and Bellona time to hijack the sentry bots and broadcast a counterfeit signal from their internal transponders.

The Doctor also reprogrammed them with a virus Jean Philippe developed, which would essentially spread to other bots that use the same core code system. Pretty soon, we'd have a small army of sentries we could connect to Bellona or Jean Philippe in case the need arises.

I'm willing to bet that body rejuve that we'll need it.

After sending the refurbished sentries back out into the wild (hopefully to infect their sentry bot friends and family), we regrouped on the Diamond's bridge to study whatever intel Jean Philippe could find.

The clock is ticking. And if the intel from both Agent Zero and Mother Ryn were to be trusted, security's going to shoot through the roof within the next 48 hours. It's going to be ugly the moment that super-secret Conglomerate delegation arrives. In which case, we'd be cooked. Extra crispy, too.

But if there's one thing I've learned, it's that I'd rather have a clear extraction plan with several exit routes. And if there's any team in the galaxy that can find those needles in the proverbial haystack of likely probabilities, it would be my crew.

That did not make the next three and a half hours any less nerve wracking or tedious, at least for those of us who have actual neurons. Even though all of my neurons are also embedded with nanoprocessors.

"So, we've narrowed it down to living quarters, daily routines and armed guard detail," the Doctor says.

"Exit routes remain problematic because we have no idea when this delegation is to make its *grande apparence*. The intel is either so good that we have effectively acquired top secret info or..." Jean Philippe says, but I interrupt before he can finish speaking.

"It's a trap. Of course, it's a trap. When is it ever NOT a trap?" I say, taking another swig of coffee. "Safest bet is for us to proceed like it is, then find more unconventional ways of exiting the station with the princesses. Nice, quiet and easy. We can't afford to put an extra target on ourselves, not while we're still being hunted."

"We're still at a thirty-two percent survival rate unless we factor in new variables. Is it absolutely necessary to not... well... blast our way out like we always do?" Bellona asks.

Everyone chuckles. I'm so fried that I actually join in.

We always try to sneak in and do any job without blowing things up. Key word "try". Mostly, we fail.

I look at all of them. My little army. They are the most advanced pseudo-organic synthoid hybrid intelligences in the known galaxies. They're also the only real family I've ever had. And that count includes any humans I've met so far.

As I look at their lovely familiar 'faces', a surge of protectiveness grips me. I would do anything to keep them out of harm's way. And yet, here we are in danger again. And for what?

"I like it when we blow things up." Mick says, drawing more laughter. Of course the heavy artillery siege bot likes blowing things up.

"We've talked through this before, Yuki. Those girls are prisoners as implied, but not in practice. They're safe as Conglomerate pawns. And you don't owe the Alliance anything. We settled that score on the day they set us free." Leon says.

My Leonidas. My shield. Always my protector. Always the strong and silent force who holds the crew together. He's also the first of the seven I discovered while bouncing about in that Conglomerate black site.

Speaking of black sites, I might as well drop this bomb now.

"This is personal, Leon. I have unconfirmed, but trustworthy intel that the delegation is coming to take the girls to the Leghrelnis station."

Silence grips the room.

"How..." Bellona starts to ask, and I answer quickly to settle any doubts.

"Mother Ryn's files. She kept it from me. From us. Why, you ask?" I pause for effect. "Because the good Admiral didn't want us on this mission in the first place."

I can feel their collective trepidation in the neuroweave. I wasn't the only one who had terrible memories of that place.

"Ryn was playing it cool with me. She didn't know what the Conglomerate would do to the girls after they were taken. Our only job was rescue them before that happens. To be fair, her reports couldn't confirm that their final destination was Leghrelnis anyway. Still, the Leghrelnis system does happen to be a major jump point from Faldan to the central systems."

I let that simmer for a bit with the crew. I'm especially sympathetic for Leon and the Doctorm who have always been the most protective of me. Leon is the more protective of the two, so I lock my gaze on him when I finally break the silence.

"And you're right." I say. "I don't owe anyone a damn thing. But these girls... They're like me. Everything taken from them. Made to live under whatever conditions the Conglomerate dictates. They have no freedom. They have no future. That's a certainty if they actually end up in Leghrelnis, where Octavia buries all her secrets and weapons. No little girl deserves that."

"Aye, but I'm willing to wager nobody's going to be cutting into their wee pretty heads and modifying their brains on a weekly basis. Pawn or no, they'll be safer than most if Faldan is to stay compliant." Doctor Capaldi says.

Anyone who didn't know him would have dismissed his words as a reprimand clad in sarcasm. But he was programmed with considerable empathy as a medical bot. Only he knew the price my mind and body paid when Octavia experimented on me.

A year or maybe two after we'd escaped, he'd had the courage to ask for adjustments to his settings. He didn't want to feel too much of what he processed during my time as the Queen's favorite lab rat. He also made it clear that the only things he would ever care about were me and this crew.

I hate to use that against him now, but this mission strikes too close to home. So close, that even as I speak of my past, I am assaulted by it.

I try to block the memories, but they come in waves.

The splitting migraines. The haze of sedation. The cold floors and processed air. The way the restraints chafed across my limbs and body as I lay shivering on the Leghrelnis worktables.

I power through the memory and continue my explanation. "I found a file that Ryn tucked away. Nothing to do with the mission, but I snooped and found more on Leghrelnis. It says the main 'workstations' have been reopened." I pause, before adding, "For the sake of these girls, I don't want to take a chance that this 'relocation plan' happens to coincide with Octavia's grand reopening of her little shop of horrors."

Pretty sure if my bots could turn pale, they all would have. Thanks to whatever tech they were built with, the same tech that's in my brain, they don't perceive the universe as ordinary synthetic minds do. And my link to them intensified their uniqueness.

They're... alive. Real.

And they're the most alive they can be when they're around me. Most themselves, the selves fully actualized, while connected to the neuroweave.

They didn't know how to process what they felt until meeting me. Until I named them. Until we achieved full interface and found a way out of Leghrelnis.

The weight of all that baggage settles on them. As we continue planning, I sense their new resolve. They were going to see this op through, whether or not they wanted.

"We're getting them out, Doctor. Captain's prerogative." I say. "This one isn't just for the Alliance. Clear?"

All seven of them transmit their affirmations. They're not enthused in the slightest, but they're certainly determined.

After we reach an accord, I looked to Jean Philippe. I could sense through the weave that he had something on his mind. I raise my eyebrows, a silent question I know he will answer.

"*La Reine* Octavia could very well be part of the secret delegation. She has all but expressed the value of the princesses as political prisoners." Jean Philippe says matter-of-factly. It's lovely and annoying how well they all know me. JP especially. "*Alor, ma fille*, you and I, we love efficiency and mischief, *no*? Perhaps you wish to accomplish as many things as possible while we are here?"

Busted. It doesn't surprise any of them, but this is their polite way of asking me what the real plan is so that they can calculate better ways to go about it. The Doctor's "face" is now so cross that I swear whatever passes for eyebrows on his visage are now on attack mode.

"Say I did want to be efficient. And let's say, an opportunity presents itself where we can gain access to high-level Conglomerate closed networks and retrieve... invaluable information to the Alliance. All while successfully rescuing persons of interest, and thus turning the tide of this war." I state my thoughts without actually saying yes to Jean Philippe's kind, yet unapologetic outing of my intentions.

"Your memories." Leon says suddenly, "That's what this is about."

"That's what this is *also* about." I counter immediately. No sense in lying to them now. "Look, I'm a lot of things, but stupid about our lives isn't one of them. If we have a clear shot, we take it. If we don't have a clear shot, we don't take it. I just want to know what the odds are."

"Six point two three three percent." Bellona chimes in curtly, with only six point two three three percent of her usual mirth. "We need a new variable, Yuki. Several new variables. Our success window is so tiny as it is. Adding a secondary parameter is suicide and you know that. Hey, here's a thought! We've actually run scenarios where—"

"No." I cut Bellona off because I know that tone and I know what she means.

I know *who* she means.

No way. In the last decade since the Alliance freed me, I have never wanted to work with or get help from anyone else but the seven bots on this ship. I'll work with others if I have to, but only if they were ordered to play in the same sandbox. And the perky excited tone in Bellona's voice, coupled with what passes for a scowl on the Doctor's "face" did not bode well for me.

Seems like they all know that and don't care. Traitors.

"Look, I don't like the swaggering bastard m'self, but if it means we escape with the wee ones alive, ye at least need to try making contact." Doctor Capaldi says patiently.

"We don't even know if he's here!" I yell. How is it that I am nine years old again with these knuckleheads whenever *he* comes up?

"Actually..." Jean Philippe starts.

I glare at him so hard, I can actually hear my teeth grinding in anger.

"Don't you dare." I say, heart in my throat and hoping against hope he's wrong.

"I was going to say that we won't know unless you hail him with an Alliance frequency." He replies evenly. "And no, I did not pick up any trace of the Sol Pernix anywhere."

At least he had the decency to ignore my outburst, even though I know he's judging me. Five hells, *I'm* judging me.

The fact that I'm both relieved and yet extremely disappointed (and maybe a *little* sad) at this update makes me hate that dolt even more.

"I am not hailing Theron Jaeger. Not even if my life depended on it." I say petulantly. And I *know* I am being petulant. Even Bellona's sensor display moved in a way that would have passed for 'rolling her eyes'.

Ah, what the hell do these rust buckets know about feelings? Human feelings, specifically.

"Well Captain, our survival rate shoots up to actual survivable levels if we involve Captain Jaeger and his crew. Which you know well from experience!" Bellona says, cheery once again.

These mutinous traitors begin their overly lively discussion about involving Jaeger and his crew. The Sol Pernix crew are all lovely, mind you. It's just their captain, and his smug... handsome... extremely punchable face that I absolutely cannot abide.

Theron this, and Captain Jaeger that. Oh, he's so resourceful! Seventy-four percent survival rate if involved from step one of the process. Blah blah blah.

"Alright, enough!" I yell. The bots go silent immediately. "You've run your calculations with complete disregard for my feelings, so let's just stick to the plans. We currently have three."

"Seven!" Bellona says excitedly. It's one of her favorite numbers and she loves having more than three plans.

"Whatever." I concede. "Mick, Iñigo, and Leon, you implement Phase Zero. Make sure everything is snug and in place. Bellona, as usual you get yourself to the highest—"

She pouts.

"Fine, you can go to the surveillance point next to the commercial district." She brightens, so I quickly add, "But the small one overlooking the central pavilion, not the giant one below the station."

"But!"

"Do we wanna talk survivability ratios? If I have to contemplate working with Captain Fancypants, you don't get to see the black market on this station. Everyone suffers." I say curtly as she keeps pouting. "Jean Philippe, we need full infiltration holos and skins for each of our entry and switch points. How are we on time? Doctor Capaldi needs at least a full four hours to bioengineer the skins."

"Three hours until all infiltration builds are fully designed and compatible with the Faldan Station systems." Jean Philippe says. "We'll make these C-suits our best ones yet."

"See if you can get Bel to crunch that down to... two hours thirty?" I look at Bellona for confirmation.

"One hour forty-five, Captain!" She says cheerily, 'hooking her arm' around Jean Philippe's and steering him towards the engineering room where they can hunker down and crunch through the builds.

"Take the boys with you. And as soon as you can, outfit them with some temporary skins for Phase Zero. We need to set things up fast." I say, watching as Leon, Mick and Iñigo follow behind the pair. "Mila, keep running scenarios, vulnerability points... whatever. Find every single way we could be killed from three thousand yards and give that data to Bellona. Both of you figure out a way we can stop that from happening."

"What say you, Doctor? Our *solnyshka* is still in denial, *no*?" Mila 'smiles' wickedly. But I know she's worried. She only teases me when she's worried.

"As the only one who shares her sentiments about Theron Jaeger, I would have to say yes. It's quite exasperating really." Doctor Capaldi quips

"*Et tu*, Doctor?" I say though I'm too tired to really argue.

The bots were there when Theron turned down my request for a spot on his ship. His excuse was that Ryn Stormcrow would be a better babysitter than he could ever be. But I had grown attached to the crew of the Sol Pernix, and I didn't want to go with Ryn. I still remember Ryn's honor guard holding me back that day as I kicked and screamed when the Pernix took off.

My crew know exactly how I feel about Theron, which is more than I'm ever willing to admit. They don't tease lightly.

"Well, if we're all about to die, you may as well tell him how ye bloody feel." Doctor C's voice is flat. I know that's his way of voicing his doubts about our survival.

"I will keep running the scenarios. You should at least call him. Better chances of survival." Mila squeezes my shoulder, a human gesture that she had apparently learned from the Doctor to comfort me.

"We don't even know if he took the job!" I yell back, half angry and half kidding about being angry.

"Admiral Stormcrow has left you without backup and with no extraction plans before. At least she was up front about it this time, which is even more worrisome." Doctor C says.

"Well, we'll just have to grab the girls before Octavia arrives." I say, committing my thoughts completely to the mission. May as well channel all these strong emotions into the keenest, toughest blade of motivation I can fashion.

"Oh, sure. Because Plan A *always* works." The Doctor says flippantly. He hands me two blue capsules. Ah, yes, blessed medical maintenance. Even in the harsh light, they glow softly. "And if Octavia does come?"

"We'll take every shot we can without compromising the mission. Simple as that." I take the pills and swallow them dry, grimacing at the faint residual taste of ozone. "Wake me in four hours, Doctor."

"Simple as that indeed." He says quietly.

I know he knows I'm conflicted. After all, we've learned our lessons the hard way. But I won't let anything happen to these girls. Or to us.

"Sweet dreams, child." The Doctor murmurs, as I head to my quarters.

Intercepted Communication Transcript
Location: Faldan Space Station, Hangar FiftyTwo

Control Tower Eight: Are you absolutely sure all the sentry bots are operational? The Commander will personally shoot us if they aren't.

Hangar FiftyTwo: Affirmative, Tower Eight. Debris dinged some of the bots on shift and scrambled their transponders. All sentries are op erational. No red flags.

Control Tower Eight: Be sure of it. Anything else out of the ordinary?

Hangar FiftyTwo: None. Well, one ship had to be rerouted from the Main Hangar to here. Big celebrity. Made a lot of noise. Said they should have had a pad in Hangar One. Said they'd complain to the Queen herself.

Control Tower Eight: Five hells. Sixteenth one today, and it won't be the last. Top brass is insisting Hangar One be kept solely at fifteen percent capacity. Why? I have no clue. Nobody will tell us anything. You get a name on this gem?

Hangar FiftyTwo: Sarlin Ha'ar. Some kind of actor or singer. Gave me and my men hell. Told 'im he'd have to take it up with the Control Towers if they wanted to lodge a formal complaint. Said he would and that his manager would be hailing the Queen within the next cycle.

Control Tower Eight: *Pfft* Performers. Next time, tell 'em to take a number and get in line. I need a new job.

Hangar FiftyTwo: You and me both, sir.

Control Tower Eight: Keep an eye on those sentries and that ship. No surprises. Tower out.

Hangar Fifty Two: Acknowledged, Tower Eight.

CHAPTER THREE

I wish I could say it was a blissful short rest. It wasn't. Too much dreaming. Some of it was memories; others were closer to nightmare scenarios. All of them tangled up in a snarled non sequitur mess. None of them from before I was seven years old.

A fun little side effect from Octavia's experiments on me is that I now effectively have more than just an eidetic memory. My memories come with high definition playback, plus sound, smell, taste and sensation isolation.

I can literally remember everything from my seventh birthday (or what I was told was my seventh birthday anyway) onwards. Anything prior to that is a complete blank— my real name, my parents, my home planet. I was constantly told that I was grown in the Leghrelnis labs and "woken up" when I had developed.

It never made sense to me. Why at the age of seven? Why not as a fully functioning adult? Whatever "science" they justified using to explain why I woke up as a child never did add up.

I guess it made sense that I circled back to this darker side of my psyche in my dreams. After all, the girls we were going to rescue were supposedly slated for a lifetime residency at the exact location of my childhood nightmares.

I'll say one more thing about these thoughts. They're very distracting when you're trying to hijack moving vehicles.

Which is what we are doing right now at the Grand Concourse, a marvel of Faldanian-Conglomerate relations in travelling infrastructure.

This superhighway connects every single sector of the Faldan space station. There were layers for travel, layers for residence, even a few tourist spots here and there, all intertwined within a physical lattice of overpasses, underpasses and roads.

All of our devised strategies had pinpointed this area as the optimal spot to begin our extraction plan for the princesses. And thus, here I am on ye auld hovercycle in whatever passes for 'broad daylight' on this station, positioned by one of the major tunnels on the concourse.

"Okay. Kill the feed in three... Two... One... And broadcast counterfeit signal." I say as the transport convoy carrying the princesses comes into sight and enters the tunnel ahead. "Cue the lights..." I add, as Bellona and Jean Philippe continue to work their magic.

I hit the gas on my hovercycle as the lights change. No other vehicles are allowed into the tunnel. On my visor HUD, I track Leon, Doctor C., Mila and Mick. They're hovering in position several meters into the tunnel, all ready for intercept. I knew those propulsion suits we snagged during the Chelnic op would come in handy. Keep flying, my pretties!

Our timing has been flawless so far.

Every day, the princesses are taken from the secure Faldan government compound to the grand communications array, so they can address the people of Faldan from a replica of the Faldanian throne room set up purely for show. Good little puppets asking everyone to drink their vita-packs and keep their heads down. Today, we timed it so we can intercept them on their way back from their daily remote "check in" with the Faldanian populace.

Jean Philippe and Iñigo already infiltrated their guard detail. They were skinned up so nicely, thanks to Doctor C. You wouldn't even think they were synthoids, let alone robots. Ah, the joys of elite tech! Note to self: these new Covert Deep Infiltration Suits are my new favorite thing.

But the C-Suits can throw you for a loop. The crew all look so ordinary and human that you'd think there'd be some cause for worry.

Fortunately, there isn't any reason to worry at all. Even if they go mucking about without their usual outer casings and armor, they aren't as vulnerable as your average human. Besides, who better to pose as armed guards than a saboteur bot and his melee combat specialist friend?

However, before Bellona can warn me, I sense a curveball through her sensors. Up to this very moment, everything was going according to plan. And it still is. I just don't know what this new variable means.

On so many levels.

"Captain. Upper northeast quadrant." Bellona signals me. I zoom in with my visor and spot him mingling among the civilians. He's pretending to be one of the many plebs taking photos of the concourse.

Agent Zero. Captain Nandru Zavus of the Galactic Defense Force Conglomerate.

You'd think an intergalactic "hero" with his star quality would have been easy to recognize. But he wasn't in uniform today.

And his hair, usually obscured by a helmet or service cap, blew freely in the wind. He even had several photocap devices to play up the tourist angle. He looked... free, I guess.

And that made me ache for a hot second.

My dumb science experiment of a brain flashed a fictional image of a woman in a sundress accompanying him. Beautiful hair, perfect skin, no scars. A clear message from my subconscious that it shouldn't be me next to him in this idyllic scenario.

Not that I'm ever ashamed of my scars, but they're generally attention grabbers of the wrong kind and make for all sorts of annoying situations. I mean, have you seen me? These scars ruin any attempt at being inconspicuous.

Anyway, I only had a few seconds left before the lights changed again, signaling the start of my bit in this op. I didn't have the time to dwell on why Z was here. Even if he'd said that he wouldn't be able to help and yet had shown up here, in this spot and this time of all the spots and times in the galaxy.

Well, here's what I apparently did have the time for: the realization that I was glad he was here.

Did it matter to me that it meant either he or all of us were in extreme danger? Nope.

Was there also enough time for my brain to remind me that, to this day, I had absolutely no idea what I wanted to do about Z and how I felt about him? Yes.

I breathe in and out, steeling myself for the next step in this op. I also push the avalanche of possibilities that explained why Captain Zavus was currently several meters from me all the way to the back of my mind. No room for any doubts right now.

The lights change and I signal the rest of the team. My part has begun, and I'm officially on distraction duty. This means that I need to do something to prevent traffic from entering that tunnel. It should be subtle enough to be insignificant to local authorities, but big enough to give us a good intercept window.

As far as distractions go, this was pretty good and easy to manage. Why, you ask?

You see, sometimes, nice big container crafts get glitchy when they're old enough. Their calcic engine arrays freeze solid when the coolant supply overflows. They screech to a halt and maintain their hover capabilities just long enough for the built-in failsafe to ground the ship safely.

And Jean Philippe just happened to find one with a delivery route schedule that coincided with the transport convoy times.

He was very proud of this fortuitous find. This craft was the right kind of bulk container and was in perfectly good shape.

I pull up to it, grateful that it wasn't a second too soon or too late. After hacking the container craft and triggering my glitch protocol, it sputtered and skidded, the momentum carrying it forward. Within a few seconds, it hovered at a standstill, drifting slightly in my direction.

Oh, what what was I, an innocent motorist, supposed to do if not 'panic'?

With the force of my technologically enhanced body, I nudged the hovercraft away from me, playing the role of a startled hovercycler. An award-winning performance, I assure you, meant for the nearby surveillance recorders. They needed to see that I refused to crash into a stalled container craft.

The vehicle continues to drift sideways, eventually taking up several lanes and effectively blocking traffic.

Task done. I deserve a cookie.

I zoom ahead, entering the tunnel at just the right pace for Jean Philippe's surveillance tech to record a clip of me. We'll remote splice it over the surveillance footage captured by the tunnel's security system via the counterfeit signal JP broadcasted.

When JP signals he has the footage he needs, I throttle the accelerator on my hover cycle and burn away the distance between me and the convoy.

Unbidden, I think again of Z and what his presence here could mean. Why has he shown up unannounced?

If this was a trap, it doesn't look like it's been sprung yet.

My thoughts sharpen back into focus when my HUD pings. It's still playing a real time holo of the shenanigans happening up ahead, though I am close enough to see it with my own eyes.

On my HUD, Bellona marked the first of the two transport crafts green, meaning Iñigo has neutralized the passengers and assumed control of the vehicle. According to Mila, the princesses weren't on board though. None of the heat signatures were tagged as theirs.

I keep pace behind the convoy and observe Doctor Capaldi and Leon as they breach the second transport.

My heart seizes for split second as I hear blaster fire from within. Three shots exit the rear panel and I silently beg the higher powers that Leon has shielded the girls and that the damage to the transport is something the Doctor can mend easily.

Two more shots erupt, and then, there's silence. Only several seconds pass, but it feels like hours.

Finally, the second transport glows green on my HUD and two of the heat signatures are marked positive for the princesses. The girls are safe.

"Targets and transports secure." Bellona sighs into the comms.

"We've got company though, but more on that later." I say for the benefit of the whole crew. "How are the girls?"

"Leon's talking to them. Telling them they'll be safe and the usual pleasantries. Now, what's this about company?" Doctor Capaldi asks.

"Agent Zero sighted. Trap's coming, if it isn't already here." I say.

"I hate traps." Bellona says immediately.

"*Capitaine*, encrypted transmission." Jean Philippe reports before he patches it through.

"Lieutenant Hersch, this is Admiral Tarr'haz. I understand you are currently en route to the compound with the princesses?" the admiral says.

Jean Philippe has already assumed control of the transport, as well as Lieutenant Hersch's identity. He responds with a brief affirmative.

"Change of plans, Lieutenant. Head straight for Hangar One and bring the princesses to the Conglomerate frigate on Dock Seven." Tarr'haz commands.

"Understand that this is highly irregular, but we have instructions from the Queen herself. Any and all changes to schedule must be cleared via specific clearance codes that she personally handed to the joint heads of security. Requesting clearance code for compliance, Admiral." Jean Philippe says, smooth as silk. The faint hesitation and feigned confidence are a beautiful touch. After all, he is speaking to a superior and requesting protocol be satisfied before his compliance.

"You're a credit to your unit, soldier. Transmitting clearance codes now." The admiral responds.

I see the codes clear on my HUD. Jean Philippe shows the Admiral his best obedient soldier face. What the Admiral doesn't see is that he has the real Lieutenant Hersch's finger pressed to the code receiver panel.

I usually have a no kill policy if it can be helped. Though I end up regretting that at times, I certainly am glad for it now. Either way, there's merit to keeping officers alive in case what you need should ever involve their live biometrics.

"I trust all is well, Lieutenant Hersch? I will be sending an armed escort to intercept you en route to Hangar One. Confirm your change in destination and chosen route so we can converge." The admiral continues.

"Bellona, given these new parameters, can you compute for which of our scenarios covers a modified escape and extraction route?" I ask. "Identify the plan with highest survivability rate."

"Plan Epsilon has the closest approximate outcome if we choose Hangar One as the extraction and exit point. It also has the highest survivability rate." Bellona supplies a beat later.

"Confirm the new route, Jean Philippe." I command.

"Affirmative, Admiral. Transmitting route changes and all possible convergence points." Jean Philippe says for the admiral to hear.

"Excellent, Lieutenant. The Queen will be most pleased. If you are fortunate, and if she is in the mood, she may thank you personally." the admiral replies.

Jean Philippe signs off. We now have approximately three minutes before the escort intercepts our route at the first convergence point.

"Well kids, this is it. I'll double back for the gear since we won't be able to pick it up." I say. "You be good at school and play nice until mommy can circle back."

I hate leaving them like this. It's not that they can't defend themselves. Even reduced to their core structures, which would roughly be the size of a young child, they are formidable on their own, even more so together. But this mission demanded some stealth, with the option of donning full gear only as the absolute last resort.

On pretty much every op, we tell ourselves that we can do away with our omega options. Well, this time, we can't afford to gamble since it looks like we're heading straight into the endgame. We may not even need the option if we work fast enough, I muse, throttling my hovercycle and taking the next exit off the concourse.

Which means I'd have to blitz if I want to be in the Hangar One area before they get there.

I exit the tunnel and take the road that leads to where we

stashed our gear. I hit an intersection and slow down to a halt. A hovercraft pulls up next to me, and my heart skips a few beats when I see who's driving it.

The look in Captain Zavus' eyes communicates a familiar urgency. It crosses my mind to do a quick check, just to make sure it's actually him.

"Day's pretty long." I say. Our code phrase.

"Hope the nights are pleasant at least." He replies. Our counter signal.

I have a split second to decide whether to tell him he's good to follow me or to buzz off. We have too many unexpected variables already. And this, this could almost be a social call. A sentiment my brain immediately and violently shuts down because there's no way he'd risk blowing his cover to say hi... right? But then again, there was that one time almost a year back.... No. Focus. Just be glad it isn't Jaeger in that craft. Oh boy, why am I thinking about him?

The light turns green. I shoot from the hip (or the heart, who knows anymore these days) and zoom off while sending coordinates to his hovercraft. His receiver's personal network is named "GunZlinger" and I hate myself for thinking that's cute.

Doing my best to refrain from further inner judgment with regards to my taste in captains, I instead opt to be glad that he chose to label his signal receiver with something directly related to our coded exchange protocols.

Soon, we are alone in the back alley where the substitute transports are cloaked. The plan was to switch transports here and retrieve the extra firepower we had stashed, before picking Bellona up on the way to the government compound. But that plan already feels like it was made three hundred years ago.

He exits his hovercraft with urgency. I am glad to see this all from my rearview monitors, because my heart is skipping beats at the sight.

I take off my helmet. I allow myself the small pleasure of feeling air on my scalp as my hair is freed from its protective prison.

"Yuki." Zavus says. It takes everything in me just to keep breathing.

"Z." I reply, playing it cool.

I push everything I feel in this moment down. Deep, deep, deep down. Easy to do for a myriad of reasons, the most obvious being that we had an op to complete. The op had to be the first on my list of immediate priorities.

The less obvious reason, however, was the short but extremely colorful history we shared. I mean... I was the one who turned him.

Or at least that's what I like to think.

Thanks to me and some carefully presented evidence, he had gotten a clear glimpse into the Queen's corrupt agenda and alliances. He'd seen what was done to me and the truth behind Leghrelnis. He even found all the other black sites. He'd broken free of his Conglomerate poster boy indoctrination after that.

The fact that he prized justice more than loyalty was something I could respect. Alright, fine, *like*. *Really* like.

I had a feeling that I wouldn't like the reason he was here right now nearly as much. I'd wager not at all. Nothing good had brought him here, and the look on his face was a dead giveaway.

"She's here. The frigate in Hangar One is hers. This entire thing was a ruse to get you and your crew back. We all played right into her hands." He states without flinching.

It's a good thing I kept my holovisor on. This way, he won't see the nanites coursing through my scars as they work double-time to scan him for lies.

I find none.

"The Queen is here." I say slowly, before adding, "How?"

"The mirror. It's been tracking you this entire time. Your crew is heading right into a trap. They've been tracking your neuroweave signals ever since you entered the system." He explains.

"And she's not tracking you?" I ask.

"She is. My cover's blown and it's only a matter of time before the mirror burns through all the false IDs I've piled one on top of the other. I've got an hour left at best, minutes at worst." He says. "It's already suspicious that you've been in contact with a civilian and are conversing in a back alley. They'll at least think I'm an Alliance operative. I wouldn't put it past the Queen to have triangulated this exact location already."

My mind races at the implications. All our Omega plans involved some kind of shoot out and mad escape. Only a handful of them involved the Queen. And an even smaller set of plans involved the Queen springing the trap herself.

None of them involved us being made out by the Magic Mirror. If I wasn't so pale already, I'm sure any color I had left would have drained from my face completely.

My concentration shatters when Bellona yells over comms. "On your six! Missiles inbound! Thirty seconds! Yuki, my position is compromised. Awaiting orders."

Icy terror floods my veins at the exponential drop in our survivability.

I take a deep breath before I look Z in the eyes. Why, oh why do they have to be so blue? Focus, Yuki, *focus.* "Trap. Okay, well, we're gonna work with that. Now, promise me that whatever happens, you will get the girls out."

"Twenty seconds! They'll be on me in ten!" Bellona yells.

"Promise me, Z." I plead.

"I promise." He says solemnly. "But how...?"

I smile. Z is predictable when it comes to his sense of justice and innate kindness. It's easy to figure out what he'll do in most situations.

In an odd moment of clarity (which always seem to come right when my life is at stake), I realize why I have the warm fuzzies for him. In a world of chaos, he's the one thing you can actually count on to be who he says he is, and do what he says he'll do. He promised me, and that means he won't let what happened to me happen to these girls.

"Plan Omega in effect. Execution code: Hide and Seek." I say into the comms, before I reach out to touch Z's cheek. He grabs my hand, sending a shockwave of... well... everything up and down the length of my arm.

I see seven confirmations blink green in affirmative on my visor. "Let's all play." I whisper to them, while drawing two hand blasters from my hovercycle's compartments.

I turn and nail the first missile at a hundred yards, but I am slower to aim and fire at the second one. It hits the pavement near us, and the shockwave takes me and Z off our feet.

Somehow I find my bearings, just barely managing to tuck and roll. Mercifully I get back up in seconds. I point my blasters at the second wave of incoming missiles, but one of them nails Z's hovercraft and the cloaked transport closest to it.

"Take the bike! Head to those coordinates! Now!" I yell at Z, while shooting at the rest of the missiles.

The sentry bots start to arrive. The first one lands on the pavement with a loud, violent crunch.

"You promised!" I yell over the noise. "They want me, and you haven't been made out yet. Go!"

I start shooting again, seeing Z climb onto the hovercycle in my peripheral vision. He'll survive this. He has to.

I need to get to the second transport in the alley. Fast.

I activate my nanites, revving up my internal processors to ensure this fight ends as quickly as possible. My neurons explode like a fireworks display, and the world slows just a little.

Two sentry bots start shooting at me, and I run right at them. I can see the trajectory of each energy bolt they fire, and it makes it easy to duck and weave to avoid getting hit.

I empty my first blaster into the nearest sentry bot, successfully disabling it. I grab it to use as a makeshift shield and battering ram against its surviving companion.

I scream as I charge, activating my personal shield.

The shield flares a bright blue, absorbing the offensive fire directed at me. I close the gap and unload my other blaster into the second sentry at point blank range.

Soon, both sentries lie in smoking heaps at my feet.

The sound of the other sentries landing in the alleyway makes me instinctively reach for the immobilizers I carry on my belt. I tug three of them free and toss them at the group of sentries that touch down in front of me, four in all with more on the way. Electrical arcs shoot out, trapping the bots in a high-intensity net of charged energy.

De-cloaking the second transport, I get in and fire it up. In the rearview monitors, I see the sentries have shaken off the immobilizers and are getting ready to open fire at the transport.

I gun the engine, clearing out of the alley as fast as I can. I really hope none of the blaster fire hits me.

"Team, Bellona is compromised. Rendezvous at extraction point omega. I repeat. Extraction point omega!" I yell over the comms. "We're taking the fight to them and it's going to be—"

Suddenly, three sentry bots land in front of the transport and fire some sort of projectile at me.

The last thing I remember before losing consciousness is the transport flipping over and me suspended in mid-air thinking, *This is going to hurt.*

MACKY SANTIAGO

It did.

Public Service Announcement
Broadcast Point: Faldan Space Station

A few hours ago, there was a disturbance in the industrial quadrant was reported. This was due to an unfortunate incident involving a container craft that was carrying several defective Jandrium cells. This commotion resulted in the destruction of a platoon of sentry bots, but please be assured that there were no life form casualties.

Your safety is always our primary concern. Should you have any queries, kindly direct them through the usual channels and we will address them as needed.

Thank you for your compliance.

CHAPTER FOUR

Story time.

There is a very unique thing I can do that makes me pretty much the best Alliance Field Operative ever. And it's not that I can mentally interface with seven elite class robots and act in concert with them as though we were a single entity.

You see, the nanites in my brain can do this thing where it allows me to remove and restore any memories of my choosing (with some pain, but not too much difficulty).

My memory repository of choice? The data cores of any one of my crew members.

Of course, I'm not a machine and my brain is not as pliant as a data storage bank. We aren't talking about ones and zeroes you can flip on and off. We're still working with neurons, electrical signals and biochemicals here. We can't delete or install data wholesale without frying my brain.

I can't just "write over" my memories and make fake ones. The nanites will pick that up and the cognitive dissonance will result in an aneurysm. I can't remove more than about an hour or two of memories without the risk of getting permanently locked in a completely vegetative state.

However, small things like, I don't know, names, faces of fellow agents I only met for a few seconds... heck, even things like secret distress signals and locations of covert Triune Alliance bases... well, those are up for grabs.

Even if you *did* have tech sophisticated enough not to scramble my brain while poking around, you won't find anything that simply... isn't there. So, slag my neurons all you want. If it's not in my head, it's not there to be found. And that basically means I can be interrogation-proof. Am I an asset in the field or what?

Hold that thought, because here's where it gets interesting.

You see, Octavia, due to her massive paranoia, built the seven members of my crew in such a way that any attempt to access their data cores by force would cause a system meltdown, effectively lobotomizing them. She apparently felt the need for complete control over the data she gathered through their systems, thus prompting her inner mad scientist to ensure that only the person in possession of the unique nanites implanted into me can access said data cores.

In her brain, that person was going to be her.

Did I mention that Evil Queen Octavia's initial plan for me was to be her disposable guinea pig? I was to be the key stepping stone on her path to becoming the galaxy's most feared and powerful weapon.

She intended to use my brain to precondition her experimental nanites, in order to enslave the wills of these seven highly advanced and specialized synthetic minds to mine. On the tail end of *that* successful milestone, she planned to liquefy my brain and harvest the nanites so she could bond them to herself.

As a concurrent failsafe, she enabled access to any of the seven data cores only when absolutely all the following conditions were met:

Requestor has fully bonded with the experimental nanites

Access is requested via the neuroweave

Requestor is doing so under their own volition with no perceivable coercion or chemical influence as verified by all seven bots

Cute failsafe.

But Octavia didn't account for my compatibility with the nanites. To twist the knife even further, she did not expect my brain to outperform hers. So when she found out I had actually bonded with all seven of her experimental bots, she just about lost it.

To course correct, she was going to scrub the bots clean and erase our "bonds", while simultaneously starting experiments on herself to bring her brain up to speed with mine. All of which would start by creating a "duplicate" access key via identical nanites she would have bonded to herself.

But we escaped before she could do it. The rest is history.

Right now though, that wasn't the part of my history flooding through me. None of those good parts where I flee my captors and find a new life for myself. No, it's just the bad parts flooding through my mind as I start to regain consciousness.

I wake to a ringing in my ears and a pounding in my head. I have been injured many times over the years and have learned to identify when there are chemicals in my system, like there are now.

As I slowly get my bearings, I notice it. More than just the expected flesh and bone sensations, parts of my mind feel bruised.

She's done a read of me! I can always tell when my memories have been accessed, and Octavia has invaded my mind just like this hundreds of times before.

My vision finally clears and I see her. Octavia the Fifth, the High Queen Bitch of the known galaxy. Well-coifed and smug, the smell of her perfume triggering too many memories at once.

For a moment, I am little again. Cold, alone, scared. Living in fear of displeasing my "stepmama".

It feels like I have gone back to being the child held captive against her will, only just learning how to ask my new friends to "hold" some of my memories so "Mama Octavia" doesn't find out we secretly played together. I lived in perpetual dread of her data extraction sessions, always deathly afraid she might find a stray memory that I was unable to hide.

Even after all this time, I am powerless before her.

Some part of my mind is screaming. I know I am not that same little girl. In fact, I am far from powerless. But I am hard-pressed to listen to that voice when fear grips my heart.

I force myself to look at her. It takes all of my strength to keep calm, to face her and stay defiant.

If not for the lines on her face and the very clear sensation of vertical restraint (as opposed to horizontal, as was the case in my childhood), I could have sworn this was Leghrelnis and a world of pain awaited me.

But I am lucid enough now to know this isn't Leghrelnis. I am, however, far from hopeful that a world of pain is not in my immediate future.

"She wakes at last." Octavia says in the same eerily soothing tone as always.

"Oh, hey." I manage to say, taking in the room. Wait, it's not a room. We're in the damned military compound, or at least it looks like a room in the compound. In a haze, I access my own memories of the compound from Jean Philippe's hack of the space station's layout.

This was a training yard, with reinforced walls and very high ceilings. It was a place where complex drills involving all kinds of tech can be conducted and contained.

Several armed guards stand at attention, including Admiral Tarr'haz. None of them wear traditional garb; they're in something spiffier. This must be the Queen's personal troop. My suspicions are confirmed when I spy the Queen's personal insignia on their uniform. Must be nice to have a private army, I think grimly.

I instinctively turn my eyes to the control room overlooking the yard. I can't zoom in and confirm for myself, but I would bet my toes the Queen's data hounds are up there.

The hounds are her personal cadre of wannabe mad scientists, parsing data and fighting for even the tiniest scraps of opportunity to ingratiate themselves with Her Royal Highness. The screams of little girls bothered them very little, and that's all anyone needs to know about them really.

Immediately, the chill of anger frosts the base of my stomach.

"If I were a sentimental woman, I would feel a flush of nostalgia at having all my children in one room like this. And after such a long time too." She says, which draws my attention to the row of containment pods behind her.

Then, I see them. All seven of them, still skinned up. They look so vulnerable. So human. Silently, I thank the higher powers that the Queen thinks them useful to her. After all, they are a treasure trove of data she could use for her mad scientist dreams to rule the galaxy. Not that she could get at them right now. At least, not without me anyway.

I could question why she doesn't consider us a powerful threat and eliminate us on the spot. But I don't. I am thankful that she is crazy enough to keep all eight of us alive.

I take a second to assess myself for any additional damage. The fact that I am coherent and have (arguably) full possession of my motor functions means she didn't try a brute force hack into my memories. *That* would have literally melted my brain. Still, I'm sure she skimmed a lot of the surface and eroded some of the mental guards I shored up.

Even with some of my memories blanked out, that's still never good for the Alliance. It's worse for me and the bots because she's now privy to everything we planned and have done so far.

It's even worse for Captain Zavus.

"Take it you've had a nice little tour of my head? You know, like old times?" I banter.

"So smug, thinking your Alliance friends have the upper hand because you can remove things from your memory." The Queen says with a sneer. She's not wrong about that; it was, after all, the one advantage we had against her.

"Though I must admit, I am glad to know that my failsafe remains flawless. Even if it is still rather inconvenient for me. So know this. When I break you, and I will, I'll have the keys to access the memory cores of your crew." Octavia continues. "And with it, the secret to how you've all managed to… what is your dreary little pet name for it? 'Achieve full interface'?"

I return her condescending smile with a scowl.

You wouldn't think it to look at her but she's completely insane. She looks more like a mother who has learned to put up with your "rebellious phase" than an inter-galactic despot lunatic. She even comes off as pleasant at first.

This side of her has fooled too many people into believing her lies about building a better galaxy.

Of course, not too many people have seen her when she's cross. Usually, it's the last thing they see, as it means you've gotten on her bad side.

"Children need a firm hand. I've always believed this. But you, my dear, have been a thorn in my side for far too long. I never really consider anything I do a failure. Not when they can be turned into opportunities." She smiles. A beat later, I hear the hiss as the large training yard doors begin to open. "Very soon, I shall be rid of you, and then I will deal with the traitors in my midst. The Alliance is wise to silo the information about their spy network, but I have a special fate planned for Captain Zavus. Now that I know he's here, it will be much much simpler. How do you feel by the way? About effectively drawing him out and thus dooming him to the fate he deserves?"

My heart twists. I know she'll make good on her threat, as she suffers no fools or traitors.

Before I can worry any more about Z, I hear heavy footfalls and the mechanized whir of elite tech. Soon enough, four synthoids stand at ease in front of us, presenting themselves to the Queen. It takes me a second look to recognize that they aren't just synthoids. Adaptive skins, the faint smell of Jandrium, the glint of what can only be Physicorum Alloy instead of skin.

This was bad news, the likes of which the Galaxy had never seen before. And I had an immediate feeling I'd be the first to find out why.

"Meet my Huntsmen." Octavia says. "The next true step in my quest to craft the perfect weapon."

The elite tech is easy to recognize. We stole enough of it when we escaped Leghrelnis. And with the crew working nonstop, we even managed to reverse engineer the crap out of it so we could design all our gear and build the Winter Diamond.

Whatever these things are, they'll be good. Even on a purely technological level, they'll be better than anything the crew and I have cobbled together. Doctor Capaldi is a bloody genius, but, even with Bellona's help, he isn't mad scientist level genius.

"I was going through a very creative phase when I made you all. You were all parts of a... pet project that I had hoped would result in the greatest weapon the galaxy has ever seen. And what do you do instead? Squander all that opportunity and potential." She rants. "Today, we shall test if my Huntsmen, void of all your flaws, will prove worthy successors and thus, can course correct some rather off-kilter variables of my life's work."

"Wait. So you got all of us in one room to test your new toys out? To see if they hold a candle to the original?" I ask.

"Don't be simple, my dear. I created you to be better than that.

So, do use that beautifully crafted brain for a moment please." She scolds lightly, like I was a child who had forgotten my table manners. "I predict my Huntsmen will make short work of you and your friends. I will then harvest your memories and your brain specifically. Finally, I will retrieve all the tech I installed. My adaptive nanites have been evolving in the last decade and have no doubt gathered an unprecedented amount of data. I am absolutely exhilarated at the chance to download what they've collected in full."

The guards set me free, just as the containment pods open with a hiss. Soon, all of us are standing in front of the Queen.

I'm not used to seeing the bots skinned up like this. Not lately, anyway, since we've had very few infiltration ops that required all of us to assume human form. Doctor Capaldi, Bellona and Jean Philippe did an excellent job. I could basically read their facial expressions just as well as I could read them in the neuroweave.

Before I can speak, the guards place our weapons caches in front of us.

"You're arming us?" I ask incredulously.

"Well. Yes. This experiment needs to be conducted within reasonable bounds. I have every interest in harvesting what I can from your collective remains." The Queen says. "This next experiment eliminates the perpetual thorn at my side and shall prove that my newest creations are superior. All in one elegant stroke. Now suit up, children. One must face the inevitable with both dignity and class."

I laugh in easily the most undignified way possible. She scowls, and it's all I can do to keep from giggling my head clean off. "Your Majesty, there are so few moments in my unnatural life that I am thankful you're a raging psychopath. This is one of them."

Silence stretches between us for a few seconds. "Make sure her brain is undamaged." She finally says. "Hounds, begin data collection."

She heads out of the room, most likely to the observation deck. She's going to want to watch her experiment succeed.

"Yuki, are you alright?" Leon asks. He looks worried, and I instinctively reach out to touch his cheek.

"I'm fine. Thank you, Leon." I say reassuringly.

A hand grips my shoulder from behind. I put my other hand over Mila's hand for a second, before I pull away and start arming myself.

"I do not like the look of those Huntsmen." She says as she loads her rifle.

"We can take 'em." Mick says as he equips all the ordnance we were given.

"They should prepare for their demise." Iñigo says, testing out his lumenblades. They had still given him four, though he only had two arms in this body.

"How are we doing on energy levels?" I ask. "You especially, Jean Philippe."

"I think I can manage. As will everyone else." Jean Philippe says.

"And the princesses?" I ask.

"They're on the way to the Hangar. I still have eyes on them." Bellona pipes up.

In my peripheral vision, I see the guards file out. They're effectively leaving us alone with the Huntsmen in the training yard.

"With any luck, Agent Zero is on his way to save the day." I say flippantly, strapping on the last of the weapons providence has granted us. I then draw both of my hand blasters. I add in a more serious tone, "We need to wrap this up. Fast."

With everyone geared up, we turn to face the Huntsmen.

"I sincerely hope you all manage some form of dignity in these …" The Queen begins to say patronizingly. She doesn't get the chance to finish her sentence.

In a split second, Iñigo has buried two of his lumenblades into the chest and temple of the Huntsman on the rightmost end of their little chorus line of death.

At the exact same time, Mila fired four concentrated bolts of mini-explosive rounds into the huntsman on the far left, blowing up its head and chest cavity.

Bellona links up with the Doctor, Leon, Jean Philippe and Mick. As Mila and Iñigo both mount a second strike, the rest of us take shelter under Leon's protective field.

I sense it before the others do. The Huntsmen that are left standing power up. This probably means some kind of energy blast is coming.

Immediately, I send a surge of warning through the neuroweave for Iñigo to retreat and for Mila to stand down.

A pulse emanates from the Huntsmen, and I know I have to do what I can to get Iñigo to safety.

"**Link Tag Protocol Activate.**" I say under my breath as I link up with Leon and Iñigo.

I use the momentum from Iñigo's assault to have him slingshot back towards us, while simultaneously extending Leon's protective field to meet him halfway. Iñigo pivots to face the radial blast from the Huntsmen and Leon opens up the protective field wide enough to let him through.

As the shockwave connects, Iñigo and I instinctively raise both his lumenblades up for protection. His blades crack upon impact. Not good.

I de-link from Iñigo and pull Bellona in so that she and Leon can throw a barrier up right where the shockwave and the blades meet.

The resulting clash of energies sends Iñigo wildly hurtling backwards towards us. Thankfully, he lands on his feet, using the blades on his soles to skid safely to one side.

Bellona amplifies Leon's capacity to concentrate power at every point on his shield that the shockwave hits.

I feel it in the air and through Bellona - the energy levels are massive. We don't have the raw power necessary to push back against this wave, not with the crew skinned up like this, armed only with their auxiliary gear. We need to dissipate this pulse or we'll be overwhelmed by it.

Bell's calculations are complete in nanoseconds. Together, she, Leon and I send out a counterpulse that dissipates the shockwave completely.

Our victory is short-lived. The fallen Huntsmen start to rise and repair themselves since, apparently, Octavia has baked some kind of nano-tech reconstruction into her new toys.

"Five hells." Doctor Capaldi says. He had only just begun his research into nano-based quick healing of severely damaged non-organic material a few weeks ago. Confirming my fears that we were outclassed on some levels. Hopefully not all.

"Jean Philippe?" I prompt.

"They're shut tight. Infinite revolving combinations. I can maybe crack the first layer in…" Jean Philippe explains, but Bellona interjects.

"Three years, at this rate. We can't get a clear hack, Yuki."

"What naughty children, playing before mother says you can. Observe how obedient my Huntsmen are. Their only directive was to defend themselves when on the brink of certain incapacitation." The Queen says, her voice echoing through the speakers around the training yard. "Now, watch and see what good little children do for mother."

There's a pause before she issues a series of commands. "Numbers one, two, three and four, subdue all eight subjects. Cripple and maim if needs be, but ensure the following parts are intact and ready for extraction: memory units of the seven assault robots, cranial nerves and cells of human female."

At her words, the Huntsmen charge toward us with frightening speed. They are formidable, and intimidating with all the shiny toys they appear to be equipped with. Energy weapons, something that looks like an upgraded version of Iñigo's lumenblades. Pulse particle explosives. Smaller energy production with a bigger bang, the kind of tech I've been wanting to get Mick for months.

"Ring-a-levio! Let's play!" I yell, triggering one of our favorite battle protocols. Leon casts the safe zone perimeter around himself, Mila, Bellona and the Doctor. Mick, Iñigo, Jean Philippe and I, on the other hand, face off against the four Huntsmen.

The four of us take our shots when we can, before fading back into Leon's protective field. We dodge, and weave, and strike. We stave off every blast and every counter-strike from the Huntsmen. As the shields open and close to allow us in and out, Mila fires shots at the targets left open in their pursuit of us. Anyone that gets nicked or dinged is healed by Doc in the few seconds we spend sheltered in the safe zone.

It's an old game that infuriates most people we tangle with. Strike. Duck back into the safe zone. Launch our attacks again, with Mila as cover fire to make sure our offensive and defensive capabilities are balanced.

But the Huntsmen hold their own. It takes far too long for me to realize that they're studying us and exploiting our patterns. They're maneuvering us in order to keep hammering away at exactly the same spot on Leon's protective field, clearly in an attempt to weaken it or use it as part of whatever battle strategy they're cooking up.

I figure it out another beat later. Because they are targeting the same spot, Leon is forced to divert power away from the rest of the shell. As the Huntsmen begin to dodge better and anticipate the shots Mila fires, I don't even need Bellona to confirm that it's time to switch strategies.

"Captain..." Bellona warns. "They'll dismantle our tactics and overwhelm us soon. We need to put them down, fast."

"Bellona! Concurrent Protocol Activate: Hopscotch-Checkmate! Omega level 2! Let's Play!" I yell.

The neuroweave floods me completely, and I don't know where I begin and where it ends. All I am sure of is that, unlike when I am consumed completely when linking with the whole crew, this protocol allows me to keep being myself while knowing exactly what everyone else is doing. It's basically like a hive mind, only this time Bellona's the queen, not me.

Immediately, I see a grid over the entire room. Each of our targets is lit up and assigned a number according to Bellona's tactical calculations.

The moment the last target is lit, we all get into position.

Leon, Bellona, Doctor Capaldi and Mila leave the safe zone as it dissipates. Everyone partners up for this next bit. I see their eyes and "faces" light up with the reddish tinge that signifies they are on full suppression mode, which is the mode for all omega level variants of our protocols.

I smile. I don't care if it's a tell that my loves are on full murder-bot mode. People usually don't live long enough to tell the tale. The ones that do manage to escape our rampage? Well, they're usually too busy dodging the blades and blasts to even remember the crimson tinge of death in their "eyes". Or mine.

"Full enemy suppression and stomp to home in five..." Bellona yells as she blocks and parries along with me, dodging whatever our target Huntsman throws our way.

Leon lunges straight for Mick's target and envelops it in a containment field. The field flares a bright silver, signifying it's basically now up to the strength of a capital ship's deflector shield. Without missing a beat, Mick jams every cannon and explosive disbursing weapon he has into the containment field and opens fire.

The room rumbles with the sheer amount of heavy ordnance Mick unloaded onto the first Huntsman on our kill list. The explosion is punctuated by the Huntsman's power core going up in flames. Bellona notes the extreme power spike Leon needed to contain the blast and how he probably only has enough energy to do that three more times. She broadcasts that in an instant and we all know we have the make the next few seconds count.

Nothing new here.

From the corner of my eye and through the neuroweave, I see/sense Iñigo and Mila issuing crippling strikes at their target while our first Huntsman smolders in a heap.

"Four!" Bellona yells as Iñigo and Mila continue their assault. They're unmatched in their precision, shooting and cutting at the Huntsman's joints and moving parts. I wish I had the luxury of time to enjoy the spectacle of Iñigo darting in and out of the Huntsman's flailing attack range while weaving in and around Mila's blaster fire.

Just as the two other operational Huntsmen nearly overwhelm us, containment fields appear to shield me, Bellona, Jean Phillippe and Doctor Capaldi, saving us from some severe damage. This also gives the Doctor enough time to repair Jean Philippe's arm, which was hanging at a terrible angle.

It's like clockwork. Jean Philippe's arm is repaired, while Mila and Iñigo deliver strike after strike in order to immobilize our second target. The Huntsman finally staggers long enough for Mick to position himself to deliver the killing blow, making both its head and torso explode.

Before the blast can flash-fry us, Leon disables the shields around us and contains it. The explosion lights up the training grounds, the blast area flaring a silvery white.

"Three!" Bellona yells as she and I rally, driving the Huntsman we were fighting back a few feet. We just need to hold this one off long enough for...

Mick, Iñigo and Mila descend on the Huntsman, raining down a hailstorm of blades, blaster fire and explosives. I can't help but grin as my murder-baby bots do what they're good at. Bloody poetry in motion, that's what they are.

I don't see it, but I catch a quick flash of silver light in my periphery, accompanied by a loud bang. On faith, I know Leon has also contained that Huntsman's fiery death.

"Two!" Bellona yells again. My insides coil in anticipation. In the neuroweave, I can feel that target three has been neutralized (with much impunity). Now it's time for the home stomp and checkmate.

As the remaining Huntsman comes at me in a flurry of energy blades, I time it so I butterfly kick one of the blades away and retreat, giving Iñigo a chance to engage it in my place.

In a fluid motion, Iñigo tosses Doctor Capaldi one of his lumen-blades while he and Mila begin their immobilization attacks. Mila then tosses the Doctor one of her rifles and then proceeds to unload her blaster's worth of energy clips into this last Huntsman.

Jean Philippe joins the fray, coming in close and striking at critical points of weakness in the Huntsman's armor and circuitry, while Mick hands the Doctor some of his smaller heavy rounds.

As the crew immobilizes the last Huntsman, Leon casts his capital ship grade containment field around it. Leon's containment field is smaller and weaker this time, as we're going to need that excess energy we don't plan to contain.

Without an ounce of hesitation, Mick and Mila blow the last Huntsman to all the five hells.

As the Huntsman's power-core hits critical levels, I break into a run, then leap over the barrier. I land on Leon's shoulders and catch the modified weapon the Doctor throws me. Quickly, Leon clips his wrist shield generator to my ankle.

"One!" Bellona yells before the Huntsman explodes.

I feel Leon create an opening in the barrier as he activates the wrist shield propelling me two hundred feet through the air towards the control booth.

When I'm about fifty feet away from the control booth, I link up with Mick and Jean Philippe. I borrow their 'eyes' so I can identify every place I need to shoot at in order to break through the protective glass on impact.

Every target lights up on my HUD.

"Checkmate!" I yell in unison with Bellona.

I open fire on the booth using the explosive rounds first. Immediately, I de-link from Mick and Jean Philippe and link up with Mila and Bellona as we fire shot after calculated shot. The façade of the booth erupts in flames.

I don't need to see through the smoke, with Bell and Mila guiding my hands and eyes. We unload the last of the explosive rounds at every fracture point Jean Philippe and Mick picked out moments ago.

Thirty feet away from the booth, I run out of explosive rounds. Whatever rounds are left in Mila's surge rifle should be enough to punch through the dura-glass that hadn't fully shattered after my first salvo.

Bellona increases my precision a hundred-fold as I open fire with the surge rounds. I shoot through the dura-glass, nailing every fracture point still lit up on my HUD. I alternate between breaking the glass and returning fire at the soldiers shooting at me. My sensors tell me that I have managed to maim or kill most of them as they struggled to protect the Queen and themselves.

I have standing orders from the Alliance forbidding me from assassinating her, but I have very little room for regret right now and absolutely no time to spare on an alternate plan. Murder in my heart, I fix my eyes on Octavia and raise my gun... only to discover I've run out of bullets.

A feral cry tears through me as I slam through whatever's left of the dura-glass and unsheathe Iñigo's lumenblade from Mila's rifle. In a flash, I register that the Queen still has a couple of guards left standing. I quickly take down these last two guards as they attempt to herd Octavia away from the broken view panels.

I de-link from Mila and link up with Iñigo to finish the job.

I cut down the first guard quickly, and I only recognize Admiral Tarr'haz when his body hits the floor.

I raise my blade for a precise cutting blow at the last of Octavia's protectors. I realize a second too late that this guard isn't bleeding at all from the shots I fired. As the blade connects with its forearm, it is met with bone-jarring resistance, the hiss of lumeneit loud and foreboding. It isn't flesh under the charred remains of his uniform; it's Physicorum. Not good.

I only have a split second to jump back and activate the shield generator at my ankle as the fifth Huntsman powers up for another energy blast.

Before it fires, the Queen reaches for the insignia on her chest and taps it. The insignia glows briefly in my vision before I take the energy blast full on. The ankle shield sputters and breaks as I am thrown out of the control room with nigh deadly concussive force.

I thank the higher powers that our tech is pretty damn good, as I black out for the second time that day.

I barely even realize that I am plummeting thirty feet to the ground before darkness overcomes me.

MACKY SANTIAGO

Public Service Announcement
Origin: Faldan Space Station

Attention. Attention.

All citizens are instructed to stay in their homes or remain confined within the public buildings they are currently in for a surprise inspection.

Though this is only a drill, we ask all citizens to remain calm and wait to be cleared individually by the Defense Force officers and synthoids.

Again, please remain where you are for your own safety until you are cleared by the Defense Force.

We appreciate your cooperation. Thank you!

CHAPTER FIVE

When your entire childhood is spent as a Conglomerate black site experiment, it's a guarantee that you'll never have a dearth of nightmares. Anyone that's survived trauma figures out eventually that they have their own personal "greatest hits" list of recurring nightmares.

If my senses were to be trusted, one such "hit" was unfolding right before my eyes. The scene is hazy, and it certainly feels dreamlike. As it continued to unfold, I hoped fervently that I truly was unconscious.

I am falling through the air... And then strong arms are holding me. I immediately think of... No, it can't be *him*. He's far away and being important. And annoying.

Instead, I see Leon. He's still skinned up, but the synthetic nano-derm peels in places on his face due to battle damage.

In the distance, there is a terrible monster. It harvests parts from its fallen compatriots and has become something more. Something stronger and deadlier than any of us could imagine. Something powerful enough to make me believe that we will not be able to defeat it.

It takes to the air, flying and shooting green fire at my friends.

My family.

They are fighting it and they are losing.

All of a sudden, faint blue light washes over everything. It affords me a moment of comfort. A brief moment where I can believe that this is just another terrible dream.

Then, I realize we're under Leon's protective field. And the pain in my joints and body thrum in chaotic cadence with the ringing in my ears. In an instant, my memory of the last few minutes comes back in full force.

Octavia's newest creation.

The fifth Huntsman. The one she kept close to her. The one that was ready for me. Stronger now after using pieces of the other Huntsmen to augment itself.

The Huntsman deploys something from its hands. It happens so quickly, and I am too disoriented to notice it sooner.

I watch in horror as the pulse particle explosion completely engulfs Bellona in flames. What's left of her torso lands on the ground with a thud.

An enraged cry erupts from Iñigo. He leaps at the Huntsman, armed with only one blade and missing an arm. The Huntsman tries to block the cutting blow.

At the last microsecond, Iñigo pulls his strike and pivots to the side. He grabs the monster's arm and tucks it towards him, allowing Jean Philippe to plunge his daggers into its side.

White hot light bursts through Iñigo's chest as Jean Philippe's blades bury themselves in the Huntsman a second time, this time through its neck and torso. The Huntsman casts Iñigo's limp, lifeless body aside like a broken doll and blasts Jean Philippe's head clean off.

Mila's battle cry drowns out my screams. She and Mick fire round after round at the Huntsman, drawing on their own power cores for energy when their weapons have run out ammunition.

The blue light around me fades as Leon heads out to join the fray. This is no dream, and the sudden assault of sound and sensations is a nightmare. I am both numb and in extreme pain.

A bright light shines directly into my eyes as gentle hands cradle my face. A faint flash of blue passes over me and I realize Doctor Capaldi is examining me.

"Bell... Iñigo... JP... five hells, he hated being called that." I stammer, trying to get up, reaching for weapons that were no longer at my belt for me to draw.

"We don't have time, child. We have to focus." The Doctor says, diverting my gaze from the battle with the Huntsman. I do my best to focus on the Doctor, but I still see the moment it breaks through Leon's protective field and stabs Mila through her chest cavity.

"Whatever happens, you need to use this only when all of us are lost. This is my last one, so make it count." The Doctor says as he tucks the last med-pen into my thigh holster. "And try to forgive us and yourself for today."

I try harder to get my bearings as I watch him head out to try and repair the heavy damage Mick has sustained. Nearby, Leon tries to hold off the Huntsman's fire. He barely manages.

Less dazed, I look around for a weapon to use to defend myself. There are none near me, and I stagger to my feet and run towards

Jean Philippe.

I stop short, horror creeping in as I realize I can't feel him through the neuroweave. I scan frantically through the weave, but I can't feel any of them. How much damage could they have sustained for them to be completely disconnected from the neuroweave?

My denial lasts only for a second. After what I had just witnessed, the simple truth of it washes over me: they were all gone.

Part of me fights, asking the right questions. I understood numbly why the others would no longer register on the neuroweave. But Doctor Capaldi? Mick? Leon, who right now was doing his best to shield the others? Nothing. I couldn't feel them at all, and I had no idea why.

But I don't have the time left to worry.

I reach the spot where Jean Philippe has fallen and seize all of his weapons. I even take the concealed wrist blasters embedded into his left arm, though it takes me a moment to figure out how to pop it free from his wrist.

For the life of me, I can't remember when he'd last modified it. He's always tinkering with the Doctor, so this must be a new upgrade. A vise closes around my heart at the thought that this is the last of the concealed weapons mods of its make I'll ever see.

I turn to run, but an explosion knocks me back a few feet. I almost black out again, but fight to remain conscious and upright.

Taking in the scene before me, I almost wished I was unconscious.

Mick was in pieces and Leon hung impaled on the huntsman's blade. Doctor Capaldi inches towards me, his midsection completely blown out, then slumps over, the light in his eyes flickering to darkness.

I cannot even begin to describe the sound that tears through me as I begin attacking the Huntsman. I shoot and slash, darting in and out of its path. I land a few blows and a few shots, but the damage heals instantly.

"You see, my dear. Stripped of your friends, you are honestly unimpressive." The Queen comments.

As I continue fighting the monstrosity that killed my family, I notice the crew status on my HUD. I would have been able to acknowledge the loss if it said terminated, but all seven of them register as status not found.

The Huntsman takes advantage of my distraction and manages to land a few blows on me.

"Frankly, you are no greater than the sum of all the parts of your unit. But don't feel too bad. That was part of your design." The Queen drawls. "So reliant on the neuroweave and on each other that you fail to function at optimal order when the weave is disrupted. Disappointing, but predictable."

So, that's her other ace. She finally jammed the neuroweave. It wasn't cruel enough that we were set up to fail. She just had to make sure we were disconnected from each other in the end.

Rage freezes in my veins. I take a deep breath and play my last card for this round. I play it hoping that my friends... my family would give me strength for this one last gambit.

"On your own, you are in no way remarkable. A brilliant

fighter, marginally intelligent, sure. Clever even. But certainly not extraordinary." She continues. "Your friends and their data cores are now mine. See how cleverly they have been dismantled?"

I shut the neuroweave off and dig deep into my mind to activate some of our omega protocols. They may be offline, but I'm not. Not yet.

"The only reason my Huntsman has not killed you is because it has strict orders to incapacitate you." She says, as I toss a few obscurers in the Huntsman's path to give me some cover.

As I activate omega protocol seven, I run towards Leon. I manually trigger his protective armor to disengage, ripping through his nano-derm skin. It immediately begins to arrange itself around me.

When the last piece affixes itself to my nape, my HUD interfaces with it and I can see that the armor is only at three percent charge. Still, I feel stronger, sturdier even.

I lunge toward what was left of Bellona's body and retrieve her processor, annexing it to the side of my head. It clicks into place and interfaces with the body armor. I feel an immediate mental boost and my mind clears up.

I dodge the Huntsman's next salvo of energy blasts and slashes as I continue my desperate scavenger hunt.

I make my way to Iñigo and Mila. I take Iñigo's lumenblade and his visor, merging it with Mila's targeting system.

The Huntsman comes at me, blades out, and I narrowly escape the attack. I have to keep moving!

With these new pieces in place, my battle senses heighten. I swear I can almost predict what this Huntsman will do a nano-second before he does it, like it's telegraphing its movements right to me.

I make my way over to Mick's torso and take his processor and whatever explosives he had left.

The Huntsman lunges straight toward me for another killing blow, but I use a full percent of Leon's armor to repel the attack with an energy field. The force sends it hurtling back towards the far side of the nearly demolished training yard.

Finally, I make it to Doctor Capaldi. I retrieve his processor, and go through his supplies to take the remnants of the reparative nanites he brought.

Leon's armor drops to point five percent power, but I have what I need. As Bellona's processor runs overtime and Doctor Capaldi's processor syncs up, I spend another point two percent of power fitting Mick's remaining ordnance into Iñigo's lumenblade and doing a full analysis of the approaching Huntsman.

I drop to one knee and feign exhaustion. I only had one chance left. And I sure as the five hells was going to make it count.

"Sleep well, child." The Queen says. Her Huntsman charges toward me to deliver his final crippling blow. "I assure you that this is not a slumber you will wake from."

At the very last moment, just as the Huntsman's blade is a milli-meter away from piercing my skin, I pull all power from the suit and channel it into the tip of the lumenblade.

Silver white fire erupts between me and the Huntsman as I thrust the lumenblade with all my might into the Huntsman's torso. The small blast sends us flying in opposite directions.

I do my best to land on my feet. With no charge left in them, Leon's armor and all the other pieces of my friends I had affixed to it start falling away from my body.

The Huntsman stands up, convulsing slightly thanks to the electrical pulse coming from the lumenblade embedded in its torso. It will have difficulty moving so long as the blade keeps emitting that pulse, which won't be for very long.

"Hmph." I barely hear the Queen say. "Very resourceful. I'll give you that much."

Pushing through the grief and the excruciating pain shooting through my body, I taunt her. "All that crap about not being 'special' when I'm all alone... That's just you projecting. I'm not less of anything with or without them. And I swear on the five hells, you will pay for what you took from me today, but I'll be damned if I don't take your monster down with me."

I run towards the Huntsman. This is it. This is the moment this gamble pays off or I die a horrible death at the hands of this lunatic. In case of the latter, I really hope I'm unconscious for it.

I reach the Huntsman with just a few precious seconds left of the immobilizing pulse and grab the hilt of the lumenblade. I force the hilt down as far as it can go, which jams the tip of the blade upward into the Huntsman's shoulder area.

With more than half of the weapon embedded into the Huntsman, I duck as low as I can and detonate the explosive core I wove into the blade using Doctor Capaldi's reparative nanites.

The explosion throws me back with such concussive force that I am winded and seeing double as I get up. I push past the white noise ringing in my ears and the double vision to tap into my auxiliary power cells. You know, the ones that keep my nanites turbocharged so that I can process information, think and act faster and better than any human in the galaxy.

I need one last boost of clarity if I wanted to put this monster to bed, just enough for a second or two worth of enhancement.

Right now, I see how its nanite-enhanced Physicorum shell has erupted into an angry mass of roiling circuitry and molten alloy. But amidst the technological chaos, I see it: the Huntsman's core circuitry.

Draining my own power cells to almost nothing, I assess within pico-seconds which key component would take the Huntsman out.

Wasting no time, I sprint towards the Huntsman again. With my remaining strength, I plunge Jean Philippe's last dagger into the nexus of connections near its energy core, disrupting the flow of power to its entire frame.

I make short work of the Huntsman's transponder with the last few charges on Jean Philippe's wrist blasters, destroying its receivers. It won't be getting further instructions from the Queen.

I disengage, but not quickly enough. Even as the Huntsman shuts down, it still jabs me in the side with a small blade.

Pain tears through me. My legs give way. Darkness creeps along the edges of my vision.

Gritting my teeth, I crawl away from the Huntsman's body. Its hulking form flails as it tries to repair itself with failing power and no instructions from its mistress.

The Huntsman manages to right itself as I continue inching backward towards the remains of my family. If I was going to die, I wanted to be surrounded by them one last time.

It seems like the Huntsman has managed to fix itself. It lurches forward, slower than before. Perhaps it's drawing on some kind of auxiliary power source?

Even without my enhanced senses, I can tell it's not even a fifth as lethal as it would have been on full power. I can also tell that with the kind of injury I have, it can execute its mistress's most recent command with very little effort.

I rummage with shaking hands for something, anything on my person that I can use against it. I see what's left of my friends, and for the first time in a long time, I feel despair. The same kind of despair I felt as a child in Leghrelnis after discovering my ultimate destiny, especially since it appeared like I was going to finally fulfill it.

Each movement was agony, and only sheer adrenaline kept me from blacking out again. I hardly even registered the Queen fussing at her creation.

In desperation, I grab hold of the med-pen that Doctor Capaldi had asked me to keep. I pulled it out of my med case, fingers trembling.

"You shouldn't be this incapacitated, cut off from your main power source... What could possibly be draining your.... Aha!" I hear the sound of tapping as the Queen fumbles with her datapad.

The pain is too overwhelming and it drowns out my horror at the sight of the Huntsman powering up fully.

"There's a good boy," she cooed. "And what an important new discovery! The neuroweave dampening field consumes ever so much power. Well... We don't need that now, do we?" She sneers as she disables the field.

The Huntsman starts towards me again just as I am about to jab the med-pen into my thigh. I want to make my last stand on my feet, and I hope that there's enough of this dose to numb my pain. I'll not go quietly, I think grimly, even if I have to use my teeth, I'll do it.

My confidence wavers for a moment when I glance at my bleeding side and the trail of blood I left. 'Tis but a flesh wound', I think, recalling some pre-galaxy era footage I watched as a child.

The Huntsman has continued to advance, but the Queen gestures for it to stop. "No, no. Let her use up the last of her little mementos."

She looks to me, her face filled with the kind expression that has fooled millions. "It's time. On your feet, then. Heal yourself and come fulfill your destiny. Besides, we can't have you bleeding out and dying before we can transport you, now can we?"

I jab the pen into my thigh as firmly as I can manage. As its contents enter my bloodstream, a streak of silver flashes amidst the bright blue liquid. Nanites, I think, but not the reparative kind.

As the liquid floods my system, I don't just feel the calming rush of anesthetics. There was something else here. Something I had asked a friend to hold for me, so I would remember it at just the right time.

"Any last words, child?" She asks.

"Sure." I say as I reconnect to the neuroweave. "Blind Man's Bluff Protocol: Activate. Let's play."

Public Service Announcement
Origin: Faldan Space Station

Code Red. Code Red. Full lockdown conventions activated.

Please remain where you are for your own safety. Civilians caught wandering outside designated enclosures will be apprehended for vio lating lockdown conventions.

Any civilians caught streaming illegal fake broadcasts or accessing unsanctioned streaming feeds will be apprehended. Repeat. Offenders will be apprehended and charged with aiding seditious activities.

Repeat. Code Red. Full lockdown conventions activated. Remain within designated enclosures for your safety.

Compliance shall be rewarded. Noncompliance will not be tolerated. Thank you!

CHAPTER SIX

As soon as I speak the words, the "bodies" surrounding me light up. The Huntsman senses danger and takes a moment to assess the situation before making his report. "Several high intensity explosives detected, Your Majesty. For your safety, I suggest—"

"I know!" The Queen seethes, reading off her datapad with the kind of fury I would have savored in different circumstances.

I mean, I'd have savored it more if I wasn't high on meds and kind of bleeding out.

Her facial expressions twist into several fun iterations. I have no doubt that, at this point, she is scanning the bodies around us in an attempt to calculate her next best move. I also have no doubt that she's found any viable options.

Bless her heart for trying.

I, on the other hand, lean back onto the nearest hunk of steel that can hold my weight.

"Hey, ma." I say with as much nonchalance as I can manage. "Lemme break it down for you, nice and quick. Although... I think you already know, so I'll just rattle it off while you stew."

She continues to ignore me. So, I rattle on, shaking with exhaustion as I rest my weight fully on the debris.

"We knew this was a trap the whole time. Gamble number one was whether you'd still go out of your way to capture us, so we prepared for that. Made sure we had leverage." I say. "Gamble number two was that you wouldn't harm the data cores, so that's where we hid the bombs. Also, fun bonus - we repurposed your sentry bots for our nefarious scheme."

She was still running scenarios and computing probabilities on her datapad. That's fine. I rather like gloating, so I go on.

"I gotta say I'm psyched that you couldn't tell that the crew were piloting these dupes remotely." I watch her lose her patience at the inevitable. "Nice touch with the neuroweave jammer though. We did not see that one coming. Although... it kind of fueled the ruse that we needed you to believe. And we all *really* needed you to believe you'd won. Because hey, nothing says 'I win' like the smoking remains of your sworn enemies."

Her face was now a mask of unbridled fury. Or rather, the mask was off and her real crazy-face was showing. *This* evil bitch I could deal with, no problem.

"I think by now you know that even if you manage to jam the neuroweave again, I've already triggered the self-destruct sequence with, oh wait, a dead man's switch. Meaning if I die, if I leave the vicinity... If I am unconscious in any way, the bombs go off. And you along with them. And... well... me. You get blown up with me." I continue. "Believe me when I say, nothing would please me more than our mutually assured destruction... Actually, that's not true. Your sole destruction would be more pleasing, but given this impasse, I'll take what I can."

"You think you've won here." says the Queen, barely containing her fury.

I *love* this day, I think giddily.

"Actually, I think you've lost. Jury's out on whatever the hell I've won." I say, then wince. The med-pen couldn't quite over-power all the pain. "Any day I stop you from doing your favorite thing is a good day."

"*My* favorite thing." She repeats, trembling.

"Yeah, you know... making life a living hell for some folks. Little girls, in particular." I say nonchalantly.

I read the data feed from my crew as they continue working on all their assigned tasks. I analyze their updates through my worsening double vision, before I pause to look my former cap-tor in the eyes. "I had a feeling you were taking the princesses to Leghrelnis. Whether that's true or not, you're never going to get a chance to do that. At least, not to those girls."

"The princesses are already within my grasp! With a simple command, I can have them spirited off to a black site even you haven't heard of." The Queen retorts, some of her trademark smugness cutting through her fury.

"New site, huh? That's interesting. About that 'within your grasp' thing though... I don't know if you're right about that." I analyze the countdown timer Jean Philippe sends me. Forty-five seconds. Oh goodie, and here I thought I would have to wait longer.

"Insolent child. Commander Ronquillous, report!" The Queen practically yells into her datapad.

Silence. She yells again. More silence.

"You might want to check the surveillance feed from Hangar One." I suggest. Her face turns fun shades of pink and purple while watching whatever footage she's receiving on her datapad. It thrills me how much she tries to keep her composure. "Pretty sure Captain Zavus has the princesses now. You know, just in case you're wondering what's happening over there."

I wince again. My vitals are dropping from loss of blood. I didn't even need my HUD to tell me that I'm going to pass out soon.

"But the Defense Force is..." She says through gritted teeth.

"Oh, you mean your extremely united forces that would have managed to take on half my crew, a couple of field agents and one defector nice and easy? Yeah. They would have totally been good if they were all in one place." I say. "You might want to check Gold Quadrant though. You'll find another wildcard at play."

It only takes a few seconds of her scanning through the surveillance feeds before she loses composure completely and throws a tantrum. It would be funny, if she wasn't a mass murdering tyrant.

Furiously, she taps her datapad, turning up the volume of the feed. A familiar voice begins to speak.

"Your evil queen is extra evil and frankly, she had all these terrible plans for your princesses. Don't you think it's time Faldan took matters into its own hands? I mean, the evidence is clear. She was going to do some crazy experiments on the girls while fooling you all into thinking she was going to take them to a more secure location for their safety. I say, fight now. Fight today! For honor, and justice and... well, because she's a just this giant power-hungry uber-cu..."

I don't hear the rest of what Theron says because Octavia starts screaming bloody murder once again. "How?? You said you'd rather die than involve the likes of him! Intelligence marked him as operating within the outer systems!"

"Please. I'm petty, not stupid. There's no way this op would have worked if he wasn't so good at what he does." I wince again, this time from admitting I needed his help and not from the mortal wound on my side. "Besides, he really is great at being a magnificent distraction. And an absolute pain in the ass."

"Distraction?" The Queen asks, suddenly hyperaware. It looks like she's finally onto the fact that there's another game afoot.

"Well, we *also* wanted to get evidence of your wrongdoings. And that takes time. So, we took said time, documented all the terrible things you've done, especially to me, and will now systematically use it against you!" I finish smugly. "Turns out, your closed network? Not as closed as you'd like."

"Nobody will believe you! I may retreat today, but know this. You've no idea the other workshops I have runnning. Places only I know the location of, places not logged onto a single data chip." She yells manically. "You think you were the last? Ha! There are others. I will raise an army of my children. Good little children. Not insolent, defective miscreants like you! I'll use every single one of them up if I have to, if it means I am finally rid of you!"

Her confession chills me and stabs a new shard of despair into my heart, but I do my best not to think of the other children she has tortured over the years since I got free. There will be time for that later, and I swear on my heart, I will deal with it personally.

"I'm sure they'll believe me after hearing *that*." I say flatly. It takes all of my remaining willpower to contain my rage. "You got all of that, Jaeger?"

He looks straight at me through my HUD. I didn't need to see the feed from the Queen's datapad because I was watching it all. On mute.

"Every single word. Been broadcasting this whole time." Theron replies, his voice clear as the feed continues streaming on the Queen's datapad.

The Queen screams as she breaks the datapad in half. Didn't think the old bird had that kind of upper body strength. She lunges at me, but her franken-droid stops her. It restrains her going on a tangent about how harming me would trigger the dead man's switch and that it was no longer a viable option for her to remain here if she wanted ensure her survival. She kept raging, completely ignoring the advice her Huntsman was valiantly suggesting.

"Hey!" I yell at her in order to get her attention. I don't know where the surge of strength came from, but I had enough to stand up. "Are you gonna kill me and end it here? Or are you going to tuck tail and run? I would end you here and now if I could, but ridding the universe of the evil you've choked it with won't be accomplished by your death. Even though I hate the orders I was given, you'll live and not be a martyr your cronies can rally the people around. They'll all know you for the monster that you are eventually, and everyone will get the chance to decide whether to follow you or not. So, will you walk away? Or am I blowing us up? Your call."

She breathes heavily for a few seconds, before her composure returns and a familiar mask of calm descends over her face.

"Mark my words, child. You will burn. You, and your friends. I know how to sever you from them now. Sooner than you can believe possible, I'll make sure the neuroweave dampening field encompasses an entire planet!" She practically spits at me. "Don't you just love how experiments help us do things better the next time? Don't think for a moment my Huntsmen have not learned from this. They'll become knives in the dark, and you and your crew won't see them coming. If there's anything my momentary lapse in judgement will leave you with, it is this fear: you aren't the only child of Leghrelnis. "

Her words wash over me and I keep my face blank. I refuse to give her the satisfaction of seeing me visibly shaken by her threat. The pretense matters to me because we both know that those words have hit far too close to home.

We both know she isn't lying, not about this. This is no manipulation. Or, if it is, it's her best one yet. If there's one thing she can't help doing, it's bragging.

Her Huntsman grabs her and blasts a hole through the roof of the training yard. I watch as he flies her out, and they are out of sight in seconds

I power down the "bombs" as soon as my sensors show that she's out of range. Good timing too, because my auxiliary power cells run out right when I disarm them.

As my HUD flickers out, I am just another regular human again. There's enough energy left to receive written messages via neuroweave and I get one from Bellona saying help is on the way.

Soon enough, a hovercraft busts through the training yard doors and skids to a halt a few meters away from me.

The doors open, and Doctor Capaldi and Bellona practically leap out. Well, whatever passes for leaping out of a vehicle for bots with no legs that usually hover in midair. The Doctor jabs several needles into me right away, each one bigger than the last. He gently lifts up my arm and begins to mend the gash at my side.

Seeing these two in front of me now, and sensing the rest of the crew through the neuroweave, I can't help tearing up. For a moment, I truly believed I'd lost them.

Bellona takes my hand and beams at me with what passes for an idiotic grin. "Looooook." She says, motioning just over her shoulder.

Theron Jaeger gets out of the hovercraft's driver's seat and walks toward me.

It has been months since I last saw his face. Jade green eyes flecked with amber. Dark brown hair streaked with a few golden strands.

I'm officially declaring that the blood loss was the cause of my lightheadedness. Yes, that's right, exsanguination.

Not the look on his face. It's the look that reminds me how he alone really knows about what happened to me on Leghrelnis. That he's the only one who saw me on those worktables.

Of course, the look on his face could have really just been genuine concern at seeing me half-dead. No extra weight from the past.

"I came here as soon as I could." He says simply. "I wouldn't have let her do anything else to you."

Yeah, I'll blame my fast-approaching death on my lightheadedness. I have to constantly remind myself I have very good reasons to hate this man. I can't remember any at the moment, sure, but I won't give him the satisfaction of thinking otherwise.

"You know I don't really like you, right? Like... at all?" I say weakly.

"Yeah I don't know about that." He says looking me dead in the eyes, as his practically dance with mischief.

Whatever. I hate him.

"Well, I know that I can't patch her up while you're both making googly eyes at each other." Doctor Capaldi says crossly. I kinda hate him too now.

Theron gently takes my uninjured arm and slings it over his shoulder. He helps me into the backseat of the hovercraft, as Bellona twirls gleefully on her way to the passenger seat.

"Patch her up good, Doc." Theron says as he starts the hovercraft. "We still have to bust out of this station. And before you get all upset again Yuki, Tala and Dropshot are on your ship. It's just a matter of fighting our way to the Diamond and the Pernix."

Encrypted Transmission
Origin: Vector 27785

Cold Snap confirmed. Repeat. Cold Snap confirmed. The Sun's rays are shining as well. Awaiting instructions.

Encrypted Transmission
Origin: Alliance Capital Ship Haven Five,
Vector 559283

Stand down, but stay on high alert. Report any material change and standby for further instructions.

CHAPTER SEVEN

I come to in a haze of adrenaline and pain. I have the nagging sense that there is something I should be doing, but haven't done yet.

It takes me a moment to realize Doctor Capaldi is stroking my hair. He used to do this when I snuck over to his containment unit as a child. His eyes dart briefly toward the front of the hovercraft, a silent gesture for me to see for myself.

Theron and Bellona are chattering away like old friends as we continue heading towards who knows where.

For a moment, it's like I'm reliving the past. It's an all too brief moment where I am an honest-to-goodness child for the first time in my life. The memory washes over me, crisp and clear. I am surrounded by new friends and found family, heading back to the Sol Pernix to celebrate completing a nice, safe job that didn't involve us fleeing local planetary authorities. There was going to be iced dessert of some kind.

The more recent experience of believing my entire crew had been decimated, and the heavy numbness in my side soured the moment. The fact that I'd be in a world of pain when the meds wore off did not help in the slightest.

The sobriety has at least allowed me to refocus on the one thing we have to do: survive.

"Hate to interrupt the soirée, but what's our sit rep?" I ask as I prop myself up.

"Ah, the princess wakes." Theron says.

I resist every urge to poke out his eye.

"You want the good news or the bad news?" Bellona chimes in.

"Good." I say instantly.

"Well, the Pernix and the Diamond are in position to extract us." She says.

I have to ask. "And the bad?"

"There's a Conglomerate blockade steadily forming outside the space station." Bellona says. "Down here, four battalions of Conglomerate defenders were deployed to block every viable exit. The largest one is positioned to guard the Queen's frigate."

"And that's bad because…" I prompt, waiting for the other shoe to drop.

"Because Jean Philippe and Agent Zero are pinned behind enemy lines. They're a Conglomerate sandwich." Bellona says.

"Eh, clever!" Theron says, patting Bellona on the head which she, of course, was eating up. Traitor.

"Well, let's have us a bite then." I sit up further, still feeling tender where the Queen's Huntsmen bruised me. "Doctor Capaldi, I hope I'm back to fully charged?"

"Wave two backup charges expended. Ye're at 100%." The Doctor replies. "That leaves you with just one last set."

"I'll make them count." I say, calling up comms. "Bellona, patch me through."

I connect with the rest of the crew almost instantly. Jean Philippe is in full stealth mode, hidden like a trapdoor spider on the Queen's frigate. Mick, Leon, Mila and Iñigo were en route to retrieve our omega upgrades - the real ones, not the decoys.

My crew aren't the only ones on the joint comms. To my surprise, I see Tala and Dropshot, as well as Walsh, Summer and Charles, and it brings a smile to my face. Certain captains notwithstanding, I adored the crew of the Sol Pernix.

"It's good to see you again, little girl." Tala says.

I beam. "It's good to be seen. How's my baby doing?"

"She runs like a dream. You ought to give Dropshot a few classes on how to run a ship." She banters back. Five hells, I've missed the sound of her voice. I always felt like I could conquer worlds with Tala Mienstrom at my side, so I am not-so-secretly pleased that I still have her respect even now.

"I'm certain that if Captain Jaeger were not so stingy with supplies and spent less on his clothes and more on the ship, the Pernix would rival the Diamond." Dropshot says. "His last purchase of Selverine Leather cost us a total of—"

"Yeah, let's try to focus here? We have a space station to escape and some princesses to rescue." Theron says over the snickers of both his crew and mine.

"You all know I hate to agree with Captain Jaeger, but in this case, I do. We need to get out of here fast." I frown as I notice who's missing on comms. "Bell, why don't I see Agent Zero linked up? You said he was with the girls."

"I did and he is." Bellona says carefully. I hope it's just because she's running diagnostics. "He's transmitting coded messages because they're pinned and keeping cloaked like Jean Philippe."

"What's his position?" I ask.

"About two klicks from the frigate, which from recent data, means that we need to break through four klicks worth of battalion." Bellona reports.

"Blockade's getting nastier out here. We're about two capital ships from full lockdown." Charles says. As a retired soldier, I know he knows what he's talking about. "Feels like old times."

"Dad's right. You have about, what, a fifteen-minute window before we're boxed in?" Summer adds. "Wish we could have been down there with you Yuki, but the captain ordered all of us to keep the engines warm."

I glance at Theron, who's busy pretending to keep his eyes on the road. I could tell from the faces of his crew that they felt it was a betrayal to me and mine that they weren't on the ground with us. As much as I hated to agree with Theron again, this was another good call. The fact that Tala and Dropshot were on the Diamond meant they had a better chance of getting away if things went south.

"Well, in the captain's defense, he did say he had a plan." Walsh says, defending his big brother as always. "You do have a plan, right Theron?"

Theron takes a sharp turn and we weave through some deserted service roads. On my HUD, I see Bellona is hard at work, no doubt navigating us through the clearest path to our next rendezvous point.

"The plan is to keep the ships running because we're gonna punch out of the hangar. All the extra cloaks we installed are going to run out right when the blockade becomes impassable, so you all have your orders to exit the system as soon as the last cloak falls off both the Diamond and the Pernix... with or without us." Theron orders.

His crew protests, but I cut them off.

"Guys," I say. "The Faldanian princesses need a way out and as heirs to the throne, we have to split them up to ensure that succession has the best chance it can get. Which means... We will make damn sure both the Diamond and the Pernix each have one of the girls before the blockade is inescapable. This is about them, okay? They're the future of Faldan and Faldan is the turning point of this civil war."

I sense it in the neuroweave right before Bellona cuts off their responses.

"Distress signal from Agent Zero. There's a Huntsman within a ten block radius of their location and it's burning through their cloaking fast." Bellona warbles in alarm.

Ice floods my veins. "Same one that tried to gut me like a fish?"

"Hard to say. But from my power readings, your guess is as good as mine." Bellona offers, sending me her findings.

I scan them, and realize that this Huntsman either got an upgrade or this is something completely different. Either way, we had to get Zavus and the girls out of there. "How much time do they have left before they're made out?"

"Five... Maybe six minutes." Bellona says.

"How many minutes until we reach their position?" I ask, checking to see if the Doctor has restocked my supplies and weapons. He did.

"Also five or six minutes." She says.

I call up the Faldan Station cityscape from memory and make some quick mental calculations.

"Right, change of plans. Mick, Mila, Leon and Iñigo, rendezvous point is now Sector Thirty-five. Theron, get us there now. Jean Philippe, can you intercept without being detected?" I ask, before drawing my weapons and using my go-to cocktail of med-kit chemicals and stimulants to get me battle ready. Doctor Capaldi's eyes narrow, but he says nothing. He hates the risks to my body, but also knows we have little choice at the moment.

"Sector Thirty-five is the nearest town square to Hangar One. It will no doubt be the most heavily guarded. Many wide-open spaces. That's the front line, *solnyshka*." Mila says over comms. I can feel her 'smiling'. She knows where I'm taking this.

"You bet it is." I say as Theron guns the engine. "Secure the omega upgrades and blitz on over nice and quick. Give me all of your ETAs." Once they do, I factor that into what I'm about to do.

"Jean Philippe says he'll manage. Patching him through to Captain Zavus now." Bellona informs us. "He's also says he sent possible escape routes to the captain, and that he has a present for you, Yuki."

"Looks like I finally get to meet..." Theron says with a smirk, but I don't let him finish..

"Stop talking. Like… Don't even finish that sentence." I say as I locate the controls for the hovercraft's roof. "You and Z split the girls up and keep them safe. We'll make sure you have a clean path to the extraction points."

"Copy that." He says. "We'll be crashing into the first wave of their patrols soon. I'm pretty sure their scouts are going to pick us up any moment now, if they haven't already."

"Oh, they'll know we're here because *I'll* tell them." I activate the controls to the roof of the hovercraft. As I wait for it to slide open, I take one of Leon's shield emitters and place it on the center console of the hovercraft. "This has enough juice for about a minute of shielding. Click the shiny red button to flip it on and off. Radius should cover the craft."

"Wait. What are you doing? Your bots aren't going to be here for at least another two minutes." Theron asks as I hoist myself up through the now-open hovercraft roof. Sweet merciful higher powers, I do love a nice breeze blowing through my hair.

"Bellona will give you the most viable place to power the craft down and standby. It's going to have a clear line of sight to the action. With any luck, they'll be too busy with me to notice you. As soon as you see a path, gun the engine and go for it. I'm leaving the Doctor with you!" I yell over the rushing wind. "Bell, activate Ri2x-W protocol and patch me through. Let's say hi."

"Hey." Theron calls out without a trace of his usual sarcasm or bluster. He doesn't even take his eyes off the road. But I know that tone of voice. It's enough to make me pause, even as Bellona reconfigures herself around my body.

"What?" I ask. Whatever he wants to say to me, I am going to make him work for it.

For the briefest moment, he looks at me and the look in his eyes makes want to lower my guard. When he gets like this, I remember how, even after everything, even after all these years, he would gladly risk his life for mine, no questions asked.

And because I am apparently a giant stupid marshmallow, I cave and nod my head. That's all he's getting from me. Fair trade, if one damned look is all he's offering. Whatever is unspoken between us will apparently remain that way. And neither of us would have too many regrets if this were the last time we ever saw each other.

He nods back, his eyes back on the road ahead. "Give 'em hell, princess." He says sincerely, not without a trace of anger in his tone.

"Not a princess." I say before Bellona and I take off.

Transmission
Destination: All Faldan Space Station Comms
Channels

Announcer One: Attention, Conglomerate battalions. This is Captain Yuki Shirogane of the Winter Diamond. My crew and I would like to formally issue a request for your surrender while granting safe passage for Princesses Lahani and Kelna Mardress.

This will be our final and only warning. Lay down your weapons, stand aside and let us through. Otherwise, we will be forced to employ every force at our disposal to safely deliver these girls from the hands of the Conglomerate.

To the rest of the citizens in this fine space station many of you are Faldanian, if not by birth, then by immigration. You've seen my little exchange with Her Royalness. Faldan is the turning point, the crux of this entire power struggle. Octavia has no right using these girls as leverage. You've seen the footage. Now it's time to choose. At the very least, encourage your people to step aside. For the sake of your planet. For the sake of these girls… For the sake of…

Announcer Two: We have several projectiles inbound. I count thirty four, Captain.

Announcer One: Oh, for fu……

Transmission Ended

CHAPTER EIGHT

I've never been good at making speeches anyway, I think grimly as Bellona and I dodge the first salvo of anti-aircraft ordnance fired at us. I couldn't decide if I was flattered that they thought they needed this much firepower to bring me and my crew down or horrified that they were this afraid of us.

As I weave through the airspace above Sector Thirty-five, I am reminded that it has an actual name: the Faldanian Memorial Square. It's a park in the middle of the city with monuments of Faldanian heroes and statesmen sprinkled all over. Would have been nice to take a tour, I think, if it weren't lined with a battalion's worth of soldiers, combat synthoids, assault bots, anti-aircraft towers and tanks. Right now, it's a veritable kill box.

Fortunately, I am pretty hard to kill.

Still linked up with Bellona, I deploy countermeasures as I analyze the battlefield. Several projectiles explode as they collide with my flares. Ok. It's safe to conclude that, yeah... they're afraid of me.

I can't help wondering who decided to prepare all this ordnance to be used against one strike team of eight. Then again, there is no strike team in the united galaxies quite like mine.

Gotta get rid of the rest of these projectiles though.

I pull out my newly charged blasters, overclock my nanites for a few seconds and lock on to each projectile heading towards me.

"Bell, patch me through to just the soldiers. All ranks." I say, shooting down every remaining anti-aircraft projectile on my tail. I smile as the counter on my HUD goes to zero projectiles in the air.

"Hey!" I yell when Bellona gives me the green light. "Can't a lady give an inspirational speech before getting blown up around here? I was serious about you Faldanians!"

My screen lights up with several warnings, sixty-four to be exact. One warning for every anti-aircraft projectile launched at me. Guess it's time for salvo number two of the day.

"So that's how it's going to be, huh? Are any of you battalion folks... Batalionneers... Soldiery army people..." I struggle to speak as I weave and dodge in midair. The ground troops open fire, further narrowing my field of movement.

"Are any of you even Faldanian?" I yell, before any response is cut off as blaster fire collides with the projectiles. The explosions send me and Bellona careening sideways. I'm going deaf from all the noise and that pisses me off even more.

"Well, if you're going to be like this..." I seethe under my breath before I finally interface fully with Bellona.

The world slows down. I calculate the number of vehicles and anti-aircraft mini towers I can take out given the number of airborne projectiles. Another second passes as I calculate my ideal flight plan.

I weave through the sky, flying right into the path of every active projectile while dodging blaster file. The projectiles lock on to me, and I string them along, making sure none of the blaster fire detonates them prematurely. I'm going to need them all.

I fly straight into the row of carrier craft, tanks, supply trucks and other large vehicles. This is by far the deadliest game of chicken I have played in a long while. It's kind of a rush, but only because I know what I'm doing.

I perch on top of the first tank nearest to me. I have to wait a few seconds to make sure the first set of projectiles lock on to my location without altering course.

My dance begins the moment I push off of the tank.

It's times like this that I feel graceful, because there's a beauty to what I do. I like the shapes my body makes while avoiding enemy fire. Keeping my body aerodynamic, while moving from one target to the next, in my humble opinion, is an art in itself.

The math behind this is probably just as magnificent if not more elegant.

I mean, come on, I'm hopping from tank to carrier to anti-aircraft tower, all while making sure the merry train of airborne explosives detonate at my last location. That's got to count as poetry in motion, right?

I am surrounded by mayhem as explosions blossom all around me. The thunderous chorus reverberates in lock-step with the whirring of my overclocked processors, helping me keep the remaining projectiles on my trail. The sounds fill me, little machines clicking and humming hard amidst the heavy punctuation of my enemies blowing apart.

I am a one-woman wrecking crew and I am doing the thing I was made to do. Sure, it's mass-destruction. But I was built to be the best at it.

I'm just glad I get to do it.

Eventually I see an opening as the explosions begin to die out. I land in the middle of what's left of their front line. Smoke billows from the wreckage of their heavy machinery. I stand up straight, and take a deep breath before I do a quick scan of the field.

I send a quick note to Theron to get a move on while the front lines are still scrambling, before I ask Bellona to patch me through to the battalion again.

"Alright. None of you let me finish my speech earlier, so let me just do a little recap. We're leaving this station with those two girls and we're leaving soon. Last chance to get out of our way." I broadcast. "Do you surrender?"

"Formation! Formation!" Some blowhard yells.

Bellona and I roll our collective eyes.

"That's a no then?" I ask.

"It is you who must surrender for the sake of peace and a united galaxy! Desist at once!" An officer - Commander Something-or-the-other - yells back.

"Can any of you even see through this smoke?" I ask.

"You are outgunned and outnumbered! Lay down your weapons and no further harm shall come to you!" He yells back.

"Hey, Captain Oblivious! We just blew up your entire front line with your own missiles. You seriously wanna play chicken with me again?" I reply.

"We have you surrounded! Drop your weapons or we will fire on you!" The voice says just as I finally see them. The smoke has lifted and, what do you know, I *am* surrounded.

"Actually... *you're* the ones we have surrounded." I say, seeing some familiar confirmations blink bright green on my HUD.

"Open fire!" Someone else yells, and an avalanche of heavy ordnance, laser fire and explosives descends upon me.

When the smoke clears, I take a moment to relish the bewildered looks on their faces as they realize I'm still alive and not even the slightest bit harmed.

I glance at my HUD. The members of my strike team are strategically positioned on the rooftops of specific nearby buildings. I turn and blow Leon a kiss for shielding us at just the right moment.

The Queen might have her army, but I have mine too. And right now, we are poised to begin a one-sided battle we warned them about. I *did* tell these soldiers that they were surrounded.

"Mick, Mila, Iñigo... How about a nice game of I Told You So. Let's play. Sub Protocol Nine." I command, activating the counterattack protocol designed specifically for claiming control of the battlefield. "And Bell, drop the beat."

Bellona's hacking tech is nowhere near as focused and powerful as Jean Philippe's, but it's strong enough break into any loudspeaker and crack most encrypted comm frequencies.

All around us music from the pre-galaxy era blares through the streets and buildings right as Mick unleashes his first salvo of heavy ordnance.

Honestly, scrambling frequencies can be boring. Usually, it's just lots of white noise and confusion and screaming while we surgically eliminate targets on the field in descending order of threat level. This way the confusion has some flavor, and I get to hear my favorite playlist. Who doesn't want to hum a little while working?

And I always admire my team while they're working.

They join the fray as the music starts. Mila and Mick provide cover fire as Iñigo and Leon rush toward us, cutting a swath of pure destruction through enemy lines.

Leon maintains his shield over me and Bell, allowing both of us to complete our recharge cycles. After all, flying around for so long while doing intense calculations takes a heavy toll on our resources. So for now, she and I have to sit tight and let the team handle things until we can get back in the game.

Mick is the closest to our location and finds his way to us ahead of the others, though Mila is not too far behind. Iñigo and Leon make a lovely contrast as they make their way over; Iñigo with his lumenblades, all four of them, his extra limbs out in full offensive mode as he cuts through enemy targets; Leon with his deflector fields angled perfectly to send anyone standing in his way flying.

Soon enough, they are also at my side, and I can feel more keenly how we're two robots short of our full crew. Synchronicity was built into all of us though, so it comes as no surprise that I get comms messages from both Doctor Capaldi and Jean Philippe the minute we resume formation.

Whatever brief joy I felt at our clockwork-like synchronicity dissolves after JP and the Doctor report. I grimace, feeding the data to the rest of the team.

"We're coming in hot, and there's only one exit corridor for both vehicles. You need to screen for us or we're all extra crispy!" Theron yells through the joint comms line.

"There's something after us. It's some new tech monstrosity Octavia cooked up." Z adds.

Of course this HUD display make it seem like these two are right in my face. Like I'm not sweating enough already! Yeah.... this is *not* the time. Gotta focus!

"Doctor Capaldi, Jean Philippe, disengage on my mark for Touchball Protocol. Did we find a way to counter their anti-neuroweave mojo?" I ask, patient as I wait for Bellona and myself to fully recharge.

"We'll be ready this time." Jean Philippe confirms. I don't even need the neuroweave to sense his glee.

Speaking of, if glee could multiply damage by the square foot, we'd all have been home hours ago given how much fun Mila, Mick and Iñigo were having laying waste to the enemy's defenses. But effective as they were, it still wasn't enough.

We need to thin the crowd, I think, and we have to confine the remnants of the enemy here. As long as that Huntsman is in play, our options are limited. Even with our carefully curated trump cards, having less hostiles on the field is the only way we can secure a safe exit for the boys and their charges.

"Team, we need to make an exit corridor for Captain Jaeger and Agent Zavus. They're coming in from theta quadrant with a Huntsman on their tail. Let's show the Queen what it's like to really, and I mean *really* pick a fight with all of us." I order. "Activating Touchball Protocol on my mark. Bell, Jean Philippe, start prepping for the hack now. I want no surprises."

Bellona disengages from my body and prepares to reassume her command center function. Leon hands her additional shield generator packs, then hands me my lumenblades. They're a model that Doctor Capaldi designed, balanced and weighted to exactly my specifications. They can tear through personal shielding and plate armor, and they also can serve as a great counterbalance to my shooting arm.

Finally, Leon deploys my spare tactical armor. The Doctor designed it to mimic Leon's own protective shell and added a few features gleaned from everyone else's tech. The suit hugs my body and immediately, I am less anxious. *This armor makes me thrice as hard to kill,* I think.

Timing it perfectly with Z and Theron's approach, I give the command. "Touchball protocol. Let's play!"

Leon charges up and throws a shield over Bellona, who hovers fifteen meters over him. She glows for a few seconds, interfacing with nearby surveillance sources. Once she accesses them, she begins her hack.

My HUD beeps with a confirmation notice. She's in. Bellona proceeds to feed the team the locations and numbers of every enemy hostile on the field.

Iñigo and I rush forward as we're receiving this intel. Mick and Mila are not far behind, providing massive amounts of cover fire. As Bellona feeds all of us the trajectory of each and every shot, Mila and Mick carve a path with their cover fire. That gives me and Iñigo a chance to find the quickest route to meet Z and Theron halfway.

I pound across the town square, already missing the speed and mobility of having Bellona fly me around. But we can't risk having her on the front lines, so, like always, we have to do this the hard way.

Alarm klaxons ring in my ear and light up on my HUD as Bellona detects incoming reinforcements. More tanks, this time of a heavier build, and several squadrons worth of soldiers and synths. Sure. Why not.

"Mick!" I yell, diverting his attention toward the incoming trouble.

I silently hope to the higher powers that if Mick can't totally decimate the incoming ground forces, he'll at least be able to take all the tanks out.

I'm cutting and shooting my way through the remnants of the battalion's first wave as I continue my sprint. From the corner of my eye, I watch as Iñigo makes quick work of the soldiers and synths in his way. Pretty soon, I've almost cleared the entire square, leaping over fallen monuments, enemies and their war machines.

Suddenly, my HUD lights up. Incoming anti-aircraft projectiles set off a new round of alarms in my ear, unnerving but certainly unsurprising. I would be overtly judgy that they aren't the homing kind if I had the time. Because I don't, I instead channel that energy into evasive maneuvers.

Trusting Bellona's telemetry with my life, I butterfly flip forward. The first two projectiles zip past my torso with roughly an inch or two to spare on either side. As the momentum pivots me towards the origin of these missiles, I fire up my nanites.

For the space of a few seconds, time slows, but only for me. I aim at the next three projectiles heading my way and open fire before my left foot touches the ground. The missiles explode behind me before I set my right foot down.

"Mila! Disengage and secure your vantage points. Mick, cover her. And both of you, take out whatever's shooting at me. They're being very rude." I cock my head to the right, allowing the sixth projectile to overshoot and strike the nearby rubble instead. My eardrums have had better days.

I don't look back as I sprint forward to catch up with Iñigo. Mick and Mila gaining some altitude, or at least positioning themselves just right, should allow them the leverage to provide cover fire for the exit corridor we were making.

I glance at my HUD to see that Theron and Z are close. In a few seconds, they'll be rounding the southeast corner onto the main avenue that feeds straight into the town square.

I can't actually see them right now, but I sure as the five hells can hear the sound of return fire and the throttling of hovercraft engines. Also, explosions. Quite a few in fact, and in rapid succession.

I sigh. Theron loves his thermic grenades.

I get rid of the last remaining enemy targets in my space and get into position. Leon stops behind me and I do a quick check to see if Mick and Mila are in place.

Nearby, Iñigo cuts through the last of the synthoids attacking him and nods. I flash back to the time he wasn't yet outfitted with the means for vocal communication, just because Octavia had no plans to do so. It was cute when I taught him how to nod, and it's still charming now.

I snap out of my reverie as two hovercrafts turn the corner onto the main road at breakneck speeds. Not too far behind them, the Huntsman tears through the city streets, making loud, terrifying crunching sounds with each step. If it had any problems keeping up, it didn't show.

I do my best to ignore the Huntsman so we can "board" the hovercrafts as they speed by. Leon and I aim for Z's hovercraft, and Iñigo aims for Theron's.

At just the right time, we jump.

In the blink of an eye, Iñigo, Leon and I are holding onto each hovercraft for dear life.

"Bell, Jean Philippe, we need those cameras!" I yell as we speed down the main street toward our exit corridor. One more knot in my stomach untangles, when the confirmations light up my HUD display.

When JP and Bellona link up, there's virtually nothing they can't hack. I mean, we broke into the space station. Hacking every camera and streaming feed in this station should be infinitely easier.

With all eyes on us, the Queen can spin this any way she wants. We're the bad guys who kidnapped the girls. We're destabilizing Faldan. Blah blah blah.

No matter what she says, none of her troops will lift a finger against us with the girls in our care. Can't risk endangering the Conglomerate's reputation. Which is great, but seeing how the troops are responding to us, both via Bellona's tracking and with my own eyes, it's almost unbelievable to me that they aren't trying stop us at all. In fact, I'm seeing... retreat patterns?

I was expecting some resistance, but for them to be making a way for us... Something isn't right.

I sense it in the neuroweave as Bellona warns us. From every direction, city lights, buildings... Everything goes dark and shuts down. Even the music we were blaring ends abruptly, and an eerie silence begins to hum all around us.

It feels like the darkness is alive. Alive and closing in on us while we speed toward our exit point.

I know Octavia's behind this one hundred percent, but this doesn't add up. Why would she cut the lights? It makes no sense to do that for a city block, let alone an entire city square.

I scan for power levels and it's not just the lights. It's everything plugged into the grid. She cut power to *everything*.

"Bell, trace how far this..." I command, but am interrupted by a terrible and now familiar sound. The Huntsman is powering up to fire at us.

"She's shut down the entire space station, except for life support and gravity." Bellona says.

That maniac. We have too few seconds to respond and we need to use them wisely.

"She's going to kill the girls while nobody's looking." I tell the team grimly.

The Huntsman reaches full charge and fires.

Emergency Broadcast
Destination: All Faldan Station devices and
receivers

Power grid down.

Please remain calm as power grid is rebooted.

Reboot to be completed in ten minutes.

Please stand by.

CHAPTER NINE

The blast hits us head on, but Leon dissipates most of the resulting shockwave. His shields hold up, but only because he is what he is: elite. That wasn't a warning shot. We would have been blown clean off the road if we didn't already know what we were dealing with.

My mind is racing. While the station is completely dark, Octavia will kill the girls and say we did it. If we wound up conveniently dead while trying to escape, that's just another plausible lie at her disposal. The next few moves will decide who wins this terrible game. And we can't afford to lose.

"The soldiers might think twice about harming the princesses, but the bots and synths won't. Ten to one, she'll kill any mutineers and label 'em collateral damage. Won't be the first time." Theron says darkly.

"We can't let this fight draw out. Not if we want to get the princesses out of here alive." Z adds. "We either need decoys or reinforcements, and I'm pretty sure I can only volunteer as decoy."

"Yeah, about that…" I say, "Jean Philippe, if we deploy the soldier bucket protocol now, what's the ETA?"

"Three minutes, but that takes me out of the fight." JP says.

Behind us, I hear the Huntsman charging up for another blast. I swear under my breath in every language I know. We need to lure this thing away from the girls.

"Run it now, Jean Philippe. Bell, guide the good captains through to the extraction points. Leon, brace for impact, but after that, stay with them until soldier bucket is in full swing. Then, you and JP rejoin the party. The rest of you, on me. Let's dance with tall, dark and ugly." I say, bracing for impact as the Huntsman fires again. "On my mark!"

The blast cracks through the darkness, lighting up the town square with an eerie green glow. It slams into Leon's shield hard enough to my teeth rattle.

"Now!" I yell, still shaken.

Iñigo and I leap with practiced grace off our respective hover-crafts and make our assault. From their positions, Mick and Mila unload shot after shot at the Huntsman.

I sink into the neuroweave for a few seconds. Not deep enough to achieve full interface, but enough to sync up better with Mick, Mila and Iñigo. I have to save energy, which means I can't afford to connect with them on this level for more than the space of one breath.

Everything slows. I feel my friends. I feel their anticipation, their eagerness to be in sync for the next wave of damage we planned to visit upon our enemy.
Just as quickly as it slowed, the world explodes back into action and we descend upon the Huntsman.

We pummel this thing with everything we have. Blades flashing, blasters and ordnance exploding... But the Huntsman barely staggers under the hailstorm we unleash.

While I expected it, it's still disturbing to see the Huntsman's nanite shell reform and rearrange itself to repair the damage we've dealt.

We circle it, relentless in our assault, diverting its attention from the two vehicles speeding further and further away.

I hear thuds as Mila and Mick finally join the battle at a closer range. They switch to short-range projectiles and explosives, leaving the Huntsman in flames and riddled with holes.

For a moment, I believe that my fears of a prolonged battle with this thing won't come to pass. That we won't have to lead it away from the transports. But any hope that we can destroy it on the spot fizzles out as it unleashes a radial concussion pulse that knocks us all back.

My vision swims. I am winded, but I get up and start shooting, as Mila and Mick do too.

The Huntsman limps quickly away from us. At this distance, I see it trailing nanites. Like a swarm transporting their quarry, I watch in horror as some of the surrounding metallic debris finds its way to the Huntsman's body as it begins to mend itself.

Of course this one was different. It wasn't just self-healing. No, this one apparently incorporated metals and who knows what else into itself, like it did earlier with the Huntsmen we destroyed.

The fact that it ignored four prone enemies instead of attempting any kills means we aren't its prime objective. *And* it's healing. Not good.

"Mick, full payload! We'll cover you during cooldown!" I command.

Mick rights himself and becomes a fountain of death and destruction, raining fire on the Huntsman. It stops moving, but I don't relax an iota.

When the smoke clears and Mick begins cooldown, all we see is a melting slag heap. It makes no sense. We *can't* have melted down all that Physicorum. I mean, Mick could, but at the expense of a few city blocks. That the Huntsman didn't explode in a way where we would need to contain the blast tells me this was not a victory.

I spot it then, much too late for comfort. Around the quickly solidifying mass, right at its edges, I see them. Cracks. Small fissures.

I lunge forward. Mick and Iñigo are quick to come to my aid, and together, we lift the heap aside and uncover a hole in the street.

It must have broken through to the lower tunnels during the barrage. And we gave it all the firepower it needed to do that.

I look around frantically for any vehicle we can use. "Leon! It's beneath you. Fully shield from below! Bell, I need you to scan for that thing! We lost it and it's coming to you!" I warn my team.

Finally, behind me, I spot a transport craft. It looks relatively intact and I run toward it. Getting into the driver's seat, I hope to the higher powers that it's functional. Mercifully, it hums to life with just a nudge of the ignition disk. I gun the engine as my strike team piles onto the vehicle from all sides.

Up ahead, we hear an explosion and the same eerie green light from the Huntsman's energy blast illuminates the street. It shoots upward like a beacon before dissolving into the dark.

Which would have been fine, if I didn't also hear Z and Theron swear and the princesses scream over the comms.

Heart in my throat, I check my HUD for life signs. I would have been more comforted to see that all life signs were stable, had it not been for the deathly silence over comms.

"Bellona! Sit rep!" I call.

No response.

As we speed up the street, the chaos erupting among enemy ranks greets us. Bots and synths try to suppress the resistance coming from the human contingent of the battalion. Not all humans, mind you, but there's enough of them causing trouble to be a distraction.

I'm willing to bet that the ones causing a ruckus are most likely Faldanians. They must really love the princesses if they're defying the Conglomerate this way. Or maybe they're just decent human beings who don't want two little girls to die.

"Guys?" I ask calmly as I can. "Someone talk to me…"

Just after we crest a small incline, I stop trying to contact the team and hit the brakes hard. The transport comes to a screeching halt and skids to the side. Just a few more feet and we would have toppled into a fissure several meters wide. No doubt this was the Huntsman's handiwork.

Not too far from where we stopped, I see both hovercrafts are powered down and on their sides. Leon has cast a protective dome around both vehicles and Bellona has taken shelter within it at ground level.

All around them, the mutinous soldiers are slowly overrun. The few synths that have managed to break through the ranks un-opposed have positioned themselves within shooting distance of the transports. They open fire on Leon's energy dome.

"Captain, we have tanks incoming. No sign of the Huntsman, but scans indicate it is immobile. The energy readings I'm picking up from it are off the charts though, and they keep spiking upwards. We can punch through any of the synths and even the tanks, but we can't manage that Huntsman and keep the princesses safe." Bellona reports. "Both transports are functional, and the captains and the princesses are coming to. They're banged up, but not concussed."

"Jean Philippe?" I ask, pushing the rising dread in my stomach down. We need that soldier bucket protocol.

"A minute and a half at least." He says. "But even if we manage to deploy..."

"Captain!" Bellona interrupts and I see it. The Huntsman. But it's not exactly the same one we fought earlier.

Now standing ten meters tall, the Huntsman hulks toward us, blocking the clearest exit to our rendezvous point with the Diamond and the Pernix. Its form bristles with discarded tech and wrecked vehicles, nanites crawling all over its new skin in frenetic green lines. Flanked by the two assault tanks Bellona warned us about, all three begin to glow as they start to gather energy for an attack.

The fact that I could smell the ozone displacement from this distance meant the energy output of that Huntsman behemoth has doubled.

No time for words. If this is the enemy's winning hand, I need to play mine.

For the second time within the last twenty-four hours, and for the last time today, I dive deep into the neuroweave and link up with all seven of my crew.

The world slows down once more and I am bathed in a galaxy of synapses, zeroes and ones. I feel the pull of everyone's collective minds and anchor them to mine, their thoughts orbiting me as I bring us into one accord.

Almost instantaneously, we are one and everyone knows what to do.

I only have about fifteen minutes of full interface, so we need to make this last gamble count.

I move in slow motion, the world around me almost completely still, the noises silenced to a distant hum. I run and jump, landing on both Iñigo and Mick's open 'palms'. They launch me forward across the small chasm with ease. I land on the other side and survey the battlefield.

The stretch of road we need to clear isn't long, but it's littered with enemy bots and synths shooting at Leon's protective dome.

I draw one of my blasters and ignite one of my lumenblades. Just before I wade into the fray, I begin shooting at the targets closest to Leon's protective field.

When the Huntsman and tanks fire, Leon will need to disable the protective field and deal with the blast. That will leave the transports vulnerable. I need to neutralize enemy units that I can't cut down in the next few seconds. With too many on the field, I reach reach deeper into the neuroweave and coordinate our attack.

While shooting, my heart thrums in time with Bellona's processors. I feed my choice of targets to the team, and we tear through them in seconds. Mick and Mila take out the targets nearest the downed transports, while Iñigo and I make short work of the targets that are a little further away.

As our shots and blows land, the tanks and the Huntsman fire pure destructive energy at the two transports.

All at once, I am pulled in so many directions.

I am with Leon and Bellona, calculating power levels and dissipation ratios in pico-seconds. We cut all power to the dome and throw the strongest counter shield we can manage at the coming blast.

I am with Mila, eliminating enemies shooting at the transports. As her targets fall, I shoot at mine. Our aim is perfect each time, the quick discharge of my blaster and the paced firing of Mila's rifle taking on a nearly musical rhythm.

I am with Mick, fighting in concert with Mila's targeting protocols. We fire heavy ordnance at precisely the right coordinates, so that each explosion takes out as many clustered targets as possible.

I am with Iñigo, eliminating the targets unfazed by the sudden wave of explosions, and disposing of them before they can shoot at the now exposed hovercrafts. We hack and slash our way through enemy synths and bots in a lethal cadence of steel and fire.

I am with Jean Philippe, playing puppet master and overclocking our systems, so we can finally see if the ace up our sleeve is worth a damn. Linked up like this, my processors clocking in sync with Bellona's, Jean Philippe crunches down on the soldier bucket protocol and completes it in half the projected time.

I am with Doctor Capaldi, taking lock and stock of our human charges, checking for concussions and fractures, healing any cuts and easing any bruises. Reinforcing windows and wind shields, just in case we find some way to use the hovercrafts.

I experience all of this in real time as the enemy fire strikes Leon's shield.

The dissipation shockwave is larger than we expected. Enemies close to the impact zone are knocked prone. Leon's shield wavers for a moment under the concussive force of whatever energy we were not able to properly dissipate.

The strike team and I make use of the commotion to push hard and clear a path to the convoy.

As we close the distance, I find myself feeling both present, but also far away at the same time. Full interface means everything happens both in real time and slow motion.

So, it is surreal watching the girls exit the vehicles with the captains because I am both in the Doctor's consciousness and standing a few feet away.

Meanwhile, somewhere in the distance, the faraway whine of elite Conglomerate tech heralds another assault. Seems like their plan is to pin us down and blow the city up around us.

My mind races as I weigh all our options, scenarios we've run versus scenarios we are creating on the fly. There are still too many of them where we end up either captured or dead.

In my periphery, mutiny among the humans is at a stalemate. A few more synths and assault bots break loose and launch an offensive attack. As one, Mila, Iñigo and Mick begin counter-offensive patterns while I continue to sift through our options.

I am everywhere at once: reviewing countless possibilities, present in every shot fired and strike made, holding up our defenses as the next energy beam is discharged.

The aftershocks feel both real and dreamlike. A faraway sensation in the face of my frantic attempt to find the clearest line of sight to our survival and escape.

One of the few things that anchor me to reality are the princesses. They are nearby, crying but trying to stay brave. I want to hug them and tell them things will turn out fine. But I am too many things all at once.

I steal a glance at Theron and Z.

Theron is busy shooting at the enemy, taunting them as he does. He's always loudest when backed into a corner. The sheer level of profanity he is shouting at such high decibel levels does not bode well. Somehow, amidst all the bluster, he manages to yell instructions to his crew. For the life of me, I cannot make out what he is saying.

Z is doing what I can't. He's calming the girls down, and reassuring them that we'll get them out. He glances at me for a second, a silent question. I give him no answers, because right now, I have none.

"We need an extraction plan and we need one now." Z shouts. "What's your play?"

"Hey Doc! Cover for me!" Theron shoves his wrist cannons into the Doctor's 'hands', and the Doctor takes them begrudgingly. I feel him evoke some of his battle protocols as he begins shooting. "We need to get to the Pernix and the Diamond. Work with me, Yuki. What are our closest physical rendezvous points?"

I rattle off all the rendezvous points and exit routes on my holo-display. Theron shakes his head. "No. *Physical* rendezvous points. Where can the ships be the closest to our location physically? Straightest lines only. Little to no detours."

In the distance, I hear the behemoth charging up once again.

I lay down the geographic points across the entire space station as instructed. Theron's eye catches on one point on the schematic. "There." He points. "Right bleeding there."

Z looks confused. But before he can comment, the third energy blast hits us and the shockwave sends debris flying our way. The girls run to Z and the Doctor takes time away from shooting to check if the girls are injured.

Theron and I are still looking at the 'sky'. We know for sure that behind the artificial atmo-panels is open space.

"You can't keep this up for much longer. We need the last of this..." He gestures toward me. "... to do something quick and big. Or we may as well give up now."

I recognize that look he gives me. Theron only ever gives me that look when I'm doing something dangerous with my nanites. Even in the chaos I can see the glow from my face as the nanites trace teal fire through my scars.

I briefly recall a time when seeing my nanites activate at the highest level made him uncomfortable. Now, everyone flinches except him.

How he even knows I'm on the last legs of today's final full interface is beyond me. And yet, I appreciate it. Funny where the mind wanders in the face of imminent capture or death.

"There's a Conglomerate blockade forming out there. We'll need to get to the ships in the next seven minutes and forty-five seconds if we want an eighty-three percent chance at escaping. Every five seconds we lose past that point, our success rate drops by six point three percent." I rattle off the statistics in perfect unison with Bellona.

"Let me worry about the blockade. Can you get us up there?" Theron asks. There's a familiar mad glint in his eye now.

If I resent him for knowing I can do a thing before I even realize I can do it, the feeling stays buried beneath the neuroweave.

What does bubble to the surface is joy.

Joy that my first and oldest human friend knows me well.

Joy that he's crazy enough to push me beyond the limits I would never venture past.

Joy that the survivability ratios Bellona kept going on and on about were indeed practical certainty as long as Captain Jaeger was involved in our core plan.

Ugh, Bell's gonna have a field day. I'm never going to hear the end of it.

"Yeah, I can get us up there. Work with the crew to secure the girls and use the hovercrafts. Then give me ETA's on the Pernix and the Diamond." I say, as a new plan forms in our collective minds. "Anything else?"

He nods and grins like a wolf, rattling off his ideas like he always did when we were children.

For the first time today, I really smile.

Encrypted Transmission
Origin: Vector 00234

Transmission Intercepted

Intercept Location: Faldanian Planetary Monitor
ing System

Transcript:

Connect to receive infrawave broadcast.

The stream... is ready to beam.

Yeah. I'm a clever boy.

CHAPTER TEN

"**Endgame conditions updated. Omega protocol three active. Execution code: Leap Frog.**" All eight of us speak in unison.

"**Let's play.**" I say, as the nanites in all our systems flash bright white streaked with crimson.

Seven power cores and one beating heart synchronize, and we launch into action.

I feel several waves of delight from the team at being reunited. Together, we sprint towards the Huntsman behemoth.

Behind me, Leon, Doctor Capaldi and Bellona work with Theron and Z to right the transports and make sure they're operational.

Iñigo, Jean Philippe and I rip into the first wave of enemy targets between us and the behemoth. Where Iñigo and I shoot and slice our way through, Jean Philippe works fast, disabling and incapacitating. He strikes quickly and precisely at the vital points of his targets, effectively taking them out of the game. It's so good to be on the front lines with him again.

Above, ahead of and around us, Mick and Mila unleash a maelstrom of cover fire, destroying enemy forces before they can go on the offensive.

Synths, assault bots and the handful of human soldiers still loyal to the Conglomerate fall in droves as we cut a swath toward the Huntsman.

Then, we all feel it in the neuroweave. Both tanks turn their weapons toward us, while the behemoth charges once more to strike at the princesses.

A very quick attempt to hack their systems remotely proves futile. They're on a Conglomerate closed circuit. It doesn't take long to see that several enemy targets in this area, including the tanks, bear the Queen's insignia, marking them as part of her special forces.

Up close and personal it is.

We split up immediately. Mick hangs behind to provide cover fire. Iñigo screens for me, while Mila screens for Jean Philippe as we charge in pairs.

As I holster my blaster and ignite my other lumenblade, Mila and Jean Philippe activate their cloaks and fade into invisibility.

I multitask with a song in my heart, observing the unseen duo wreak very visible havoc on the enemy forces standing between them and the tank they are targeting. My heart soars a bit higher as their tank loses the ability to get a lock on either of them, its turrets and guns lurching from left to right but unloading nothing.

Meanwhile, Iñigo and I change strategies, opting for speed instead of mass destruction. With Mick and Bellona connected to us, it's easier to pick targets and disable their long-range attack capabilities. Nobody we hit can shoot at us after we get past them, leaving them open for Mick to pick off at his leisure.
Like Mila and Jean Philippe, our goal is to get to the tanks.

Unlike with Mila and Jean Philippe's tank, however, ours has no trouble targeting us. The challenge is in actually hitting us.

It doesn't.

Nor can it. Over and over, it tries, but Iñigo and I are too nimble, dodging fire and even exchanging targets as we move evasively.

As we close the distance between us and our quarry, the behemoth remains just as indifferent to us as when we last engaged it. It charges up again and the smell of ozone displacement is so thick I can almost taste it.

It fires once more. From a distance, Leon slams back just as hard.

I see on my HUD that Jean Philippe has made contact with his tank. So have I.

It takes a few seconds to find a decent place to plant our breaching tech, but we find it. I'm just thankful we didn't have to crawl underneath these things. With the tech planted onto our targets, we all disengage and fall back behind the behemoth.

We take a moment for me to scan its weapon systems to identify where best to strike.

Before it can fire, Iñigo and I jump up on either side of it, slicing along its arm cannons and cutting them off from the Huntsman's power source. Mila and Jean Philippe remain hidden.

"Must you be so difficult all the time?" Octavia's voice emanates from within the behemoth.

Iñigo and I ignore her and carve up the Huntsman's behemoth shell, hamstringing it and severing as many of its cobbled augmentations from its main body as we can.

Octavia goes on and on. "Disappointment in..." Blah blah blah. "Your plans will not come to fruition..." Blah blah. "I'm a megalomaniacal genius and I am better than you. I'm so awesome." Blah. "My Huntsman is invincible!" Etcetera, etcetera.

As a testimony to its superior technologies, the Huntsman heals up faster than we can inflict critical damage to it. Which is mostly fine because all of this is a lovely distraction.

"You shall be crushed under the superior power of my forces!" Octavia continues to rant.

"Force this." I smile as Jean Philippe and I complete our hack of the two tanks. Immediately, we swivel all guns and cannons toward the Huntsman, unleashing every ounce of firepower they have at the behemoth.

"You dare!" Octavia screams. I can practically hear her facial muscles twitching.

"Child, you are outnumbered. What little advantage you have gained, you yourself have lost by your own hand." Octavia yells as the behemoth shambles to strike at us. It's looking like a melting heap of scrap and weaponry, less mobile but certainly no less lethal. "Why must you persist in being so exasperatingly... persistent?!"

"First of all... it's fun." I yell back, jumping and dodging and still in control of my tank. "Second of all... you sure you have us outnumbered?"

From a distance, picking up speed and getting louder by the second, I hear the roar of sentry class robot thrusters in the very high hundreds. At least, it sounds like it's in the high hundreds. My HUD says there are certainly much more than that.

The sentry bots we hacked into and now control descend from the sky and flood the streets of the square. Instantly, they turn the tide on Octavia's forces.

With the mutineers now possessing the upper hand, my HUD shows a massive amount of enemy synthoids and assault bots dropping off the battlefield.

In the neuroweave, I hand control of my tank to Jean Philippe and wrap my consciousness around Bellona's. I fall back a bit and take a turn playing puppet master to this army of sentries.

It would have been lovely... if Octavia weren't fighting me tooth and nail for it. Whatever army of codebreakers and hackers she has on retainer are doing their best to wrest control of the sentries back.

Fortunately, Jean Philippe left a series of nasty little nested loops and redundancies that change the integrity of the source code we implanted every twenty-five seconds. Eventually they'll get through, but not soon enough to stop us.

"You think you're so clever, don't you? Thwarting me at every turn this day." The Queen seethes.

"Pretty much." I say, as the sentries I control disable the last of the ground forces assembled at the town square.

Nearby, my strike team contains the behemoth.

"Your bravado means nothing. Your show of force is temporary at best. You are trapped here and I will harvest my property from your corpses soon enough." Octavia threatens. "The wise and rational choice is to surrender now."

I sense Bellona's smug satisfaction before she gives me the signal that Leap Frog protocol is ready for phase two, which is actually a hack of the entire space station.

Thanks to the inroads Jean Philippe had made since breaking into the station, Bellona was able to find her way to the inner workings of the station undetected. Full interface gives her just the right amount of leverage she needs for a hack of this kind.

With much delight, I work with Bell to disable the station's gravity generator. With the generator completely in our grasp, we deploy more of Jean Philippe's little hacking traps so we have control over the system for as long as we need.

Smiling, we shut the gravity generator off in Sector Thirty-five.

"What... what is... Well, take control back, you fools! Move you imbec....." I overhear the Queen yell before her voice cuts out.

As we all begin to float, I quickly reinforce my control over the sentry bot army using Bellona and Jean Philippe's combined processing capacity. They move like a swarm, taking orders from their queen, the role of which being played tonight by yours truly.

I command cadres of them to escort both hovercrafts upward, serving as thrusters and honor guards, guiding them swiftly toward the atmo-panels we've earmarked as extraction points.

"E.T.A. two minutes, Yuki." Tala broadcasts from the Diamond.

"Cloaks are gonna be toast in roughly that that time, so you gotta blitz now!" Walsh chimes in.

"Just be ready for us!" Theron replies over comms, which I am thankful for since I'm too busy controlling the sentries.

I command some of them to grab Mick and guide him to the front end of this zero-grav cavalcade, giving them instructions to get him to the atmo-panels well ahead of the rest.

Concurrently, I have another handful of sentries escort Leon up to hold the rear so he can still shield both hovercrafts properly. I see the Doctor and Bellona follow suit and keep pace, relying on their own thrusters for lift.

To absolutely nobody's surprise, the behemoth cobbles together some sort of makeshift thrusters that gives it limited mobility in zero gravity. I send about half the sentry bots in my control to drag it as far away from our new extraction corridor as possible. I instruct them to hit all the vital spots we identified and hit them hard.

I command the remaining bots to escort me and my strike team upwards. As they lift us up, I make sure they position me facing the roiling mess of sentry bots and Huntsman nanites disappearing slowly from view.

Of the many gambles we made today, this was the one I doubted the most.

We ascend in silence, my heart hammering in my chest. A beat later, we lose our line of sight to the hulking behemoth.

Doesn't mean I can't hear it though.

The faint echoing sound of energy blasts and sentry bot laser fire reminds me that I cannot relax until we're out of the Faldan system and back in Alliance controlled space.

Suddenly, the ruckus quiets down and a chill grips my belly. I knew there was a chance this gamble would go south, knowing what we know about this thing. But this is sooner than we'd hoped. Higher powers help us this is too soon!

A blinding flash of green light suddenly flares in the distance, followed by four concentrated bursts of energy.

All four beams slam straight into the convoy. If we weren't linked in full interface, Leon wouldn't have managed to strengthen his shield to capital ship levels in time. And since the attack came as a surprise, we couldn't compensate to make sure we kept our trajectory set.

On impact, both vehicles are knocked back as a very large, very lethal monstrosity roars its way toward us.

It's a horrifying sight. It has quadrupled in size, adorned with the broken shells of several hundred sentry bots. Their thrusters line its back, legs and arms, giving the behemoth the kind of maneuverability that would mean the death of us in zero-grav.

I only have a minute left before I collapse and the team knows this. We can't fight this thing. Not in mid-air. Not like this.

It's going to get to the girls and take us apart at its leisure.

"Mick, Bell... Help me!" I yell into the neuroweave as I get an idea. I push hard, desperation fueling my next proposed move.

I sense the slightest hint of resistance from them, Bellona especially, but I insist and give the command. With one last push, I command every sentry bot to max out their thrusters.

Mick acquiesces and blows up the atmo-panels earlier than planned, unleashing the higher end of his destructive ordnance. The shockwave knocks us back for a half second before the cold vacuum of space sucks us out of the space station.

Before I lose consciousness, I plead with Bellona to activate the emergency atmo-panels the moment the girls are out. I am too far away from the breach and the space station must be sealed before the Huntsman can get through!

With the last few seconds I have left in full interface, I see both hovercrafts clear the breach, the strike team hot on their heels.

Dread fills my heart as the behemoth speeds toward us. I yell for Bellona to shut the breach, but my voice is sounding further and further away from me.

I can only watch in silent horror as the countdown to my full interface limit clocks down to zero while the behemoth charges up for one final blast.

Darkness creeps along the side of my vision and engulfs me completely as the Huntsman overtakes me and fires.

Emergency Broadcast
Destination: All Faldan Station devices and
receivers

Alert. Sector ThirtyFive breach secure.

Gravity wells nonfunctional. Emergency tethers deployed.

Repeat. Sector ThirtyFive breach secure.

Please stand by for power grid reboot and gravity well reinstatement.

CHAPTER ELEVEN

My eyes jolt open when my tac suit deploys a shot of stimulants into my blood stream. Full interface knocks me out completely, but does nothing bad to the rest of the crew. They retain echoes of my consciousness in their systems and are extra intuitive for a few minutes more after we disconnect. I, on the other hand, am incapacitated because I'm alone in the neuroweave and need to be brought out of it slowly to prevent tissue damage.

Numbly, I float and watch the blur of activity unfold before me. Leon's shield flares a bright silver as the behemoth Huntsman pummels it with energy blast after energy blast. Then, just as it starts charging up, it takes fire from both sides as the Winter Diamond and the Sol Pernix approach. Its colossal size has made it possible for mid-sized battle ready freighters like the Diamond and the Pernix to get a target lock.

A traction beam pulls me slowly toward my ship as the Diamond and the Pernix take the behemoth down a peg or four. Both ships pummel the behemoth hard and the tide turns quickly.

"Slag the damn thing! Give it everything you have!" Theron yells over comms as the barrage continues.

Eventually, both ships cease fire. In my current immobilized, state, the only body parts I can move are my eyes and not without much strain. But I can see the update on my HUD. There are no power readings coming from the remains of the behemoth, now drifting several meters behind me.

I float in silence for a spell, drifting slowly toward the Diamond. Suddenly, there is comm chatter as Leon disables his shields and both ships open their cargo bay doors for ingress. Bellona and Doctor Capaldi board the Pernix and the Diamond while more traction beams emanate from both ships to pull the rest of the crew and the hovercrafts into the bays.

Without warning, twin beams of energy erupt from the remains of the Huntsman and slam into both hovercrafts. Both vehicles and their cargo erupt into flames, exploding while the Pernix and the Diamond open fire once again. I am still too deep in the neuroweave, not lucid enough to properly register the implications.

My comms are a cacophony of anguished screams and angry cries as Mila and Bellona integrate themselves into the targeting systems of both ships. They lock onto the smaller remnant of the Huntsman.

"Too late. Far too late once again." Octavia broadcasts on several comms channels we have kept open for monitoring. "Had you left well alone, those girls would have lived quiet, peaceful lives in the heart of the Conglomerate. But you just *had* to force my hand. Now they, along with your captains, are dust. Their demise is your fault."

Just as she finishes speaking, the Argent Fatale, the Queen's sleekest, most powerful capital ship and her personal transport, warps in behind the Diamond and the Pernix, along with several other capital ships and battle cruisers.

I spare a quick glance at my HUD. My counter for the most optimum time to warp out of the Faldan system has elapsed by two minutes. The Conglomerate blockade is now at full force.

The crew of the Pernix hurl obscenities and curses over comms, but Octavia mutes them.

"It is only out of sheer self-control and my superior proclivity to wisdom that I do not obliterate you all this instant." The Queen says. "No, too much has been wasted today and now, you see what a little patience can yield.

The princesses are now martyrs by your hands and you will all be executed for treason and murder. The Conglomerate need not know that Captain Zavus is a filthy traitor. He can continue to be a symbol of hope for the people, serving me even in his death. That Theron Jaeger will also be dead is a personal delight I will cherish."

"You monster! You were going to hold the princesses over Faldan, using the people's loyalty to the royals as leverage. You marked them as pawns in your game and damned them to a life as tools for intergalactic blackmail." I croak weakly.

"No, child! It is you who damned them! Your antics on the Faldan Space station will mean I may even have to sanitize the population. You have wrested it from my grip for but a heart-beat." The Queen seethed. "They had to die the moment you played your hand and you have lost. *You* are the monsters here today, coming in from the farthest reaches of space to upset the beautiful peace we have established in this system."

"Anyone who can blow up two little girls with the flip of a switch is a monster, you evil hag-bitch." I slur a little, but speak with conviction. "Your pet creation might have opened fire, but it was you pulling the trigger. You claim you do all of this out of wisdom, but really you're just the biggest psychopath in the known universe."

"And yet all I hear are the fruitless words of a dead girl. Nothing more." The Queen says in that smug tone of hers that makes me want to claw out her eyes. "It is by my wisdom, my restraint, and yes, my own might that I am now in possession of *you*. I have the perfect story to tell my loyal subjects and my superior intellect has secured my victory this day."

"Well, if you're so bleeding smart, how come you fall for the exact same thing over and over?" Theron says over comms. "That's right, Planet Faldan. You heard it right here! Broadcasting live. I mean, with so many people on the station who totally loved part one of today's broadcast, we figured we'd give you guys a copy of it *and* live stream part two!"

"What is the meaning of this?" The Queen sounds confused.

I manage a small smirk, so small that I barely feel it. It's highly possible my facial muscles haven't moved, but I don't care. Sometimes, you just gotta savor your joy on the inside and let the outside follow in its own time.

"Don't just like and subscribe to the 'I'm an evil psycho' channel. Show us you like it by, oh, I don't know, taking control of your planet and maybe throwing up some kind of reverse orbital bombardment?" Theron continues with mock insouciance. "You know, to knock these invading forces right out of your planetary space."

But this next line he delivers with so much conviction that I would've had goosebumps if I were fully functioning. "It is time the Faldanian Fire Sparrow left the shadow of the Imperial Nighthawk to fly sovereign once again."

Every once in a while, I am reminded why Theron Jaeger is the captain of the Sol Pernix. This moment is one such reminder.

"How are you doing this?" The Queen yells. She's starting to sound frantic now. "What cheap chicanery is this?"

"Wow, clearly, you never had a real childhood with playmates, and magic tricks and... imagination, huh. Like... ever." Theron says. It's more a statement than a question. "I mean, that's sad but it also has an expiration date as far as excuses go."

"You will explain this insolence—" The Queen is interrupted as one of the capital ships fires at the Argent Fatale. You can almost imagine the stunned look on her face as she tries to understand this next wave of fresh hell. Within the space of a few seconds, another one of her capital ships fires at the Fatale.

"Did I mention I was broadcasting this entire time? Like from the moment your Huntsman blew up the floor from underneath us down at the station?" Theron says, tone laced with mischief. "And I took the liberty of beaming all the footage to every capital ship in orbit. Gotta say, Jean Philippe and Bellona really are elite. If I never thanked you for your craftsmanship, let me express my gratitude with a little song."

Of all the songs he could have picked, he chose the most ribald and disrespectful shanty about the Queen. The same one that she had specifically outlawed throughout the Conglomerate. In between lines, Theron issued orders for his crew to reel us in, while asking Leon to standby and shield both ships.

Even in my post shutdown state, I know that Leon won't last too long against a capital ship of the Fatale's caliber, let alone an entire armada. Definitely not after this long, drawn out battle and not even with the supplies we have left on the Diamond.

I survey the chaos unfolding before me and can't help but think that even if we don't survive today, the sheer amount of damage we've would set the Conglomerate back decades with the

Faldanians.

Well, I thought it would be decades, but it seems we won't have to wait that long for Faldan to formally express their distaste for Conglomerate rule. All around me, I see the Royal Faldanian Armada, fresh from clearing Faldan's upper atmosphere, open fire on the Conglomerate blockade. That certainly gives credence to my theory.

I'll be damned. The Fire Sparrow is in open rebellion.

I don't see the rest of the battle though, as the traction beam finally draws me into the Diamond's hold safely. Soon, I find that I am once again in Doctor Capaldi's capable hands.

"He's laying it on a little thick out there, isn't he?" The doctor says, administering the rest of the meds I need for a full recovery. I try to reply with a snide comment, but he shushes me. "Plenty of time to tell that insufferable blowhard what we think of him later. And if the Queen manages to blow us up before then, I'll patch you through to him m'self."

"The girls..." I croak.

The Doctor smiles, or what passes for a smile in his case anyway.

"Kelna. Come help." Doctor Capaldi beckons. From behind him a pair of very round, curious eyes meet my languid gaze. If the younger princess was with us, then Lahani was on the Pernix.

As she takes instructions from the Doctor on how best to medicate me, I notice she has a knack for the healing arts. With any luck the Faldanian royal family will recognize this as a strength and not a skill beneath their noble status.

"Was it scary flying around in space?" I ask hoarsely.

She shakes her head. "Captain Zavus kept me safe the whole time." She adds shyly, blushing.

If I had the strength to sigh and roll my eyes, I would have. Hard same, kid. Hard same.

Before I can ask, Doctor Capaldi answers my unspoken question. "He's in the weapons bay with Dropshot and Mila. He's a good one. Too bad ye don't feel nearly half as much for Zavus as you do the other one."

I'm lucid enough now to protest, but the Doctor administers another round of meds to stabilize me before I can speak. "Batter me all you want later. For now, you need to cool down."

I fight hard to stay awake and reach for one of his syringes. You know, so I can poke him in the face. But even the thought of it wears me out and I feel myself slipping into unconsciousness.

"Ye've done yer part. You're no good to us catatonic and you *will be* if you push too hard too soon. Ye aren't so far gone that you forget we've worked with the Pernix before." The Doctor strokes my hair. "Trust us to finish what we've started."

With my limits exceeded 'ever so slightly', I have no choice. Everyone's in good hands with Theron. He'll make sure to finish the op.

With that last thought, I drift into the long deep darkness of sleep, the only surrender I allow myself this day.

Encrypted Transmission
Origin: Vector 27785

Motherland has broken the yoke.

Repeat. Motherland has broken the yoke.

Requesting clearance to assist further.

Encrypted Transmission
Origin: Alliance Capital Ship Haven Five

Copy that. Standby for emancipation protocols. ETA ASAP.

CHAPTER TWELVE

I wake to the harsh light of an Alliance med bay. Too many things come into focus all at once. Jarring as the sensory overload is, it at least tells me a few things.

The most important thing is that I have recovered completely from interface exhaustion. Otherwise, I wouldn't be able to focus on or process this many details concurrently.

Which leads me to the second most relevant bit of knowledge I can glean: I am on the Haven Five. I'd recognize the way it hums anywhere. Plus I have been confined to these exact quarters before.

My mind replays the last several hours worth of memories. Over the years, my brain has learned to do this on reflex. It allows me to ground myself in the present, to get my bearings and sift through what matters and what doesn't. On a more useful note, it helps me formulate the right questions.

Like, for instance, what's happened to Faldan and the princesses? What has the council decided to do with Z? Is the crew of the Sol Pernix still onboard the Haven? What should I do with all the information Octavia disclosed?

I sit up and am grateful that the world doesn't spin around me when I'm upright. Relieved as I am, it also tells me that I must have been unconscious for at least a day and a half. Any less time, and it's vertigo city for me.

Carefully, I remove the needles in my arm that connect my bloodstream to what I am sure are some very helpful fluids. Unless I'm in battle, and most certainly not while I'm in any kind of medical space, I don't tolerate needles in my body. Had enough of that as a child. Don't need any more if I can help it.

Like clockwork, the door to my room opens. I was expecting some ward nurse to check on the dislodged fluids, so I'm surprised to see Mother Ryn standing in the doorway.

Lady Stormcrow herself. Alliance Admiral, and one-time foster mother to one traumatized orphan and her seven elite robot friends.

"Hello, Yuki." She says with a smile.

"Hey." I nod at her. "No flowers? No get well soon holos?"

She smirks and glides over to my bedside. So stately, this one. I never did absorb any of that grace.

"You did it." She says simply.

"Go team." I reply, deadpan. Nonchalance keeps Mother Ryn on her toes and hides the fact that I'm glad she's proud of me. She isn't always forthcoming with the praise, but I've come to know her pretty well over the years. It's her eyes. She can't hide anything with those eyes.

"Of course, many Faldanians thought you took a terrible risk baiting Octavia. We're managing the few dissenting voices who want to sanction you publicly for reckless endangerment." Ryn continues.

I roll my eyes, and the look in hers echoes the same sentiment.

We both don't care and are glad for the win.

"Tell me, since when have Doctor Capaldi and Bellona had exo-suit capabilities? And just how did you manage to hide the fact that they were carrying not just the girls, but Captain Jaeger and Agent Zavus as well?"

I smile smugly. I'm very proud of this.

"You're gonna want to thank Harlan and Pirsi for that. The few times we docked here in the last several months, we got to thinking about how Bell and Doctor C's mobility tech were wasted on just simple movement." I explain. "A few missions back, we figured out that Bell would be the perfect extraction suit if we modified her to interface with my tac suit. Modifying the Doctor's frame in a similar way would be perfect for med-evac, if you keep thinking along those same lines."

She nods, easily following my train of thought. Harlan Farrin and Pirsi Klai-un were the hardware and software engineers assigned by the Alliance to care for our operative team ever since we were rescued. They also handle a couple of other heavy hitters, like the Lightning Storm and Aurora Teams. Bet Ryn's feeling a lot of vindication now after all the crap she had to put up with to get the Alliance's top team of hybrid code-breaking grease-monkeys to work with us.

"Doctor Capaldi, genius engineer that he is, found some way to make enough room for both him and Bellona to wrap snugly around both girls and captains." I continue. "The Doctor also used our spare gear to make sure they were all outfitted for exo-extraction from the waist down. Lots of jimmying involved, but we bought them enough time to get it done."

"But how did you fool everyone into thinking the girls were in the transports?" Ryn asks.

My grin is feral as I explain. "Well, first, we got JP to rig some kind of counter beacon to transmit two life signs per hovercraft. That was the easy part." I pause for effect. "Of course, we couldn't have their legs dangling from beneath the Doctor and Bellona and giving the game away. Luckily, Mila and Jean Philippe both have spare camo-cloaks. And by then, since Bell and the Doctor were technically glorified extremely high-end jetpacks, we figured we'd cover up their legs with the cloaks to make it look like Bell and the Doctor were flying solo."

We had some good plans. I don't even mind sharing credit with Theron. He floated the idea of better decoys after all. But only if people ask. Ryn didn't so... why bother mentioning?

"So, you strap both captains along with the princesses to Bellona and Doctor Capaldi... and use the transports as decoys."

Ryn shakes her head and looks at me. In moments like this, it feels she either wants to slap me or hug me. Probably a little of both.

"We needed proof that Octavia wanted to kill the girls and that she would, if given the chance." I say slowly. "We were also gambling with the fact that Octavia is obsessed with keeping me and the crew alive. Personally, I think it's because she's a big honkin' bag of crazy. I didn't think she could get nuttier, but..."

I stop when Mother Ryn takes a long breath. She learned to do that pretty quickly, just a few weeks or so after adopting me. And I've learned that when she does this, it's an effective way of asking me to get straight to the point.

"Anyway, we figured that her need to keep all eight of us alive meant that the safest the girls would ever be was in direct proximity to any of us." I say with conviction. "Leon could have shielded the hovercrafts, sure, but we had no idea what surprises Octavia had left. So, the safest thing to do was give her a target to shoot at and keep the girls in a place she wouldn't shoot at. Bell and the Doctor were just the most viable solutions. I mean, I would have preferred them to have been with Leon, but he has no evac upgrades. Maybe we should outfit him with some. Hmm..."

I draw up schematics in my head, intrigued by the idea of devising a full set of search and rescue upgrades for everyone.

Mother Ryn disrupts my planning as she starts to clap slowly.

I beam at her shyly, taken aback by her applause. Ah She's just soft on me because I helped win her back a planet. I'm also very cute. And did I mention how awesome I am?

"It seems the Winter Diamond has struck again." Ryn says, obviously proud. "Hard. Fast. Living up to the unit designation we granted you all those years ago. Not as clean and as efficient as we had hoped, but the results are undeniable."

I breathe in, before I sigh. "Hurray for Team Cold Snap?"

"I'm serious, Yuki. Angry Faldanians aside, the council wants to award you, Captain Jaeger, his crew, and..." She says, mischief in her eyes, "Agent Zavus with the Alliance cluster."

She's got a look I recognize all too well. Ooh, don't start with me woman. Matchmaking is beneath you.

"So I take it no one's too bummed that their double agent's been made out? Nobody's scared he's actually a triple agent?" I push back, shifting the topic a little.

This is the Conglomerate poster boy we are talking about after all. The literal face of the enemy for too many members of the Alliance. For at least a decade and change, when the Alliance thinks Conglomerate, his is one of the faces that immediately comes to mind.

I'm not into politics, but awarding this man a medal for just one successful op won't sit well with a lot of factions within the Alliance.

"No, they are not afraid." Ryn says evenly. "I am among the few who have their reservations about Agent Zavus formally joining our ranks."

"Shocker." I quip, fully reclining again. If she was going to talk and be cryptic for a while, I might as well get comfortable.

"Do not mistake my caution for distrust in his motives. He risked everything working with us. His actions during this last op are to be commended. Especially because it helped us Liberate Faldan." Mother Ryn says, her eyes dancing again.

A smile blooms on my face slowly. Hot damn. Faldan is free. They liberated themselves. We just gave them the nudge they needed and kept their reason for fighting the good fight safe.

Well, Theron did most of the nudging.

And hey, props to the Alliance, who I am sure helped kick the Conglomerate out of the system. I mean, the Faldanian Armada is no small thing, but the Conglomerate blockade had enough heavy hitters if I recall correctly, which I always do. Ryn must have showed up with the rest of the fleet. Kudos.

But like an idiot, I still need to know what her issues are with Z.

"So, what are you worried about?" I ask.

"That his integration into our ranks would prove too much of a distraction for our top operative." Ryn says. "The council were thinking of appointing him as secondary liaison to the Diamond and having him take on a more... permanent place on your ship. With your permission, of course. You both have worked extremely well together on the field, and it only made sense to keep the team together."

I sit up again, gearing up to say something witty and biting. But as I open my mouth to speak, I only manage to close and reopen my jaw. Ryn laughs. I snort and flop back down.

"The guys are gonna have to vote. Gotta have majority or it's a no go." I say petulantly. "And if the council vetoes any decision we come to, I will pull the 'full interface ain't gonna work unless I get my way' card so fast, it will make your heads spin."

Threats are not beneath me, even hollow ones, especially when I am feeling cornered and am only wearing a paper gown. Which is totally unnecessary by the way since I had no real injuries. Well, unless you count that one moment when I was impaled on a blade. I mean, did I die? Pfft.

Before I can protest, the door opens and Z walks in. Where's a good Huntsman when you need one?

Ryn has adopted her 'speak of the devil' expression, and I glare daggers at her. I had forgotten how much I hate that extra smug look. And I just know she wants to stick around to watch.

Before I can say anything, I'm interrupted by the synthoid voice that warbles from her wrist comm. "Admiral Stormcrow, incoming transmission for you."

"Don't you have, like, a revolution to run elsewhere?" I add without missing a beat. "Shoo. Don't come back unless you have cookies."

She smiles again, and it's the kind where she knows she has something on me. "Calliope, redirect incoming transmission to the bridge. Heading there now." She says into her comm.

"Agent Zavus." She says to Z on her way out of the room. Z nods back curtly, still a very good soldier.

Ryn gives me another brief look before she leaves us alone. I do not give her the satisfaction of seeing that I'm flustered.

Also, I will leave a Trillian swamp toad in her shoe before I leave Haven Five, just for old time's sake.

"Did I come at a bad time?" Z asks quietly.

"Depends on who's asking." I say, still trying to hide how flustered I am.

"So who's asking?" He counters.

"You tell me. You came here. This whole conversation? Totally your idea." I say, my defenses going up.

He smiles, and laughs a little. My heart begins to race. And ache. This is the man who can disarm and subdue two squadrons of armed soldiers with just a stick and his bare hands, and yet he has somehow managed not to let any of that touch him.

I, at least, have the neuroweave and seven other minds to shield me from the brutality it takes to do what I do. He doesn't have that kind of buffer. And yet, for all his lethal capabilities he remains... tender. And safe.

I never understood how that could be. Maybe I never will.

And to really make things interesting... Sitting here with him, for the first time, truly free of the Conglomerate's grip makes me think of all the questions we had for each other that we said we'd put on hold while he was playing both sides.

Questions that I still don't have answers to.

"It feels so good." He says, and I know he believes it. But is it though?

"I'm sure." I somehow manage to reply.

"Oh. Uh... I'm sorry. That was insensitive of me. Your injuries were so severe. I can't possibly imagine..." Sweet merciful higher powers, help me. Why do I love it when he sputters like this?

"Please, like you've never been shanked by a hyper experimental uber-bot with dead eyes?" I say, finding my center as I slide into being glib and dismissive. "You have your own little collection of mortal wounds and look at you all alive and... stuff. I'm good. And I'm glad you feel good because nothing beats being free of that garbage fire of an evil empire Octavia runs."

"Yeah." He says, still smiling from ear to ear. "I mean, it's terrible, but I'm free. Finally free. I can do anything I want now. Be anything I want. Fight for whatever and whomever I want."

"You really can." I say, grinning back at him.

"So, who..." *Five hells of Margh.* "I mean, what are you gonna do now?"

Someone kill me. Like, now. Please.

"Hiiiiiiiiii!" A voice calls out as the door opens once more.

"Oh." The newcomer says as her face falls. Just from that look, I know in my bones Z is the last person she wanted to see at my bedside.

"Bellona, hello!" Z greets her. He's genuinely pleased to see her. "This is a really good skin."

"Isn't it? I like it too. Thank you! Yeah." Bell say, somehow managing to sound both saccharine and curt. "But we really do want to check up on Yuki, and by we, I mean the crew."

She gestures to the open door. Leon, Mila, Mick, Iñigo, Doctor Capaldi and Jean Philippe all file in one after the other. They're all skinned up because this helps the humans adjust better to them. In their actual bodies, they're walking weapons. The skins, at least, gave the Alliance visual cues to see that they were more than just that.

"Bellona, for the last time, there's no need to..." Doctor Capaldi says with a scowl. But Bell is quick on her feet to escort Z out. I don't know if I want to hug her or throw something at her.

"Now now, Agent Zavus, Doctor's orders! We'll send word when she's ready for visitors, okay? You're such a good.... captain! And I really do like your hair!" Bellona says as she ushers him out the door. "Remember, don't call us! We'll call you!"

"Sure! Do you know my—" Z says, but he's cut off when Bellona hits the trigger for the door to close.

Mila just shakes her head, while Doctor Capaldi rolls his eyes. Leon and Jean Philippe look embarrassed by Bell's behavior, while Mick and Iñigo pretend to find something interesting on the floor and the ceiling respectively.

"*Alor, ma fille*, we should get an award for not hacking into Haven Five's systems to care for you ourselves remotely." Jean Philippe says jokingly. "We are, how do you say, the soul of restraint."

"Yeah, you should. I have half a mind to have the council bestow the Alliance Cluster on all of you. Every last one." I smirk back at him. "I mean, if everyone on the Pernix is getting one, you should too."

"Humans are peculiar about their awards, *solnyshka*." Mila says. "There are still too many who can barely accept us for what we are in these skins. I do not think bequeathing a human award to us would sit well with most."

"Have I ever mentioned that you are a major downer?" I ask Mila, only half kidding.

"I'm not wrong though." She counters.

"Also true." I say and let out a deep sigh, allowing myself to sink back into the pillows. "So... Looks like we won."

"Yeah, we did." Leon says. "Just wanted to be here the moment you woke up. We all did."

"Fairly easy task, since none of them can block our access to the neuroweave." Doctor Capaldi adds. "We knew the exact moment you opened your eyes."

"We wanted to make sure you were okay." Bellona says. "And I mean, really okay."

"You guys aren't usually this..." I begin to say, wondering why they were doting on me more than usual. But then I see it all over Leon's face. And the Doctor's. "Oh. Right. That."

I scan their 'faces', realizing that no facial expression can truly capture what someone feels. Guilt. Anger. The kind of concern that aches so bad it can only come from love. But I knew. I felt it all. The neuroweave is funny like that.

"It isn't worth much, but I did ask you to forgive us, child." The Doctor says.

"You saw us die. Your pain had to be real if we wanted Octavia to believe she'd won." Bellona says sadly. "I mean, it all went according to plan, but just the thought of..."

"Well, it was my idea." I said, overwhelmed as always at how much they all cared.

"I don't care! You shouldn't have had to have lived through that!" Leon says indignantly. "She's taken so much from you already!"

I trace lazy lines over the scars on my palms. What could I say to that? Even if it wasn't true, in the end Octavia had managed to make one of my nightmares come to life. Not only was I cut off from my family, but I also saw them destroyed at her hands.

"I'm not one for all that space hocus pocus, but even I consider it providence that we were cut off from you in those moments." The Doctor says. "We would have stormed that compound and ruined the plan had we felt what you did."

"I would have blown up every last one of them." Mick says angrily.

Iñigo stares at me, murder in his eyes.

"Well, you are all the soul of restraint." I say, tears welling up. I felt it all. How it tore them up inside. How shaken they were at being disconnected. "Well, thanks to Jean Philippe, Octavia's going to try harder to disconnect us next time.

"I can assure you her efforts will be unsuccessful." JP offers.

"Look, I made the call, and you guys did your part magnificently. All of you." I pause for a moment, choosing my next words carefully.

"Yeah, Octavia managed to hurt me again. And though it's technically my fault because I allowed myself to be in that situation, it didn't make it easier for any of us." I continue. "But for better or for worse, I learned something new and very important. Even when she took you all from me, I didn't break. I didn't freeze up. I didn't shut down. I didn't go insane or go berserk. If anything, that was the best fight of my life."

Doctor Capaldi smiles, a fierce kind of pride glinting in his synthetic eyes. Soon, they all realize what this means to me.

"That was one of the worst things she could have done to me and I survived it long enough to show her that she can't break me anymore." I say. "So how's that for another win?"

They all grin at me. They get it. They don't have to like it. Leon and the Doctor certainly didn't. But we take what we can.

And we do.

Tensions ease and the Doctor approaches the machines monitoring my life signs.

"Well, looking through this chart, you'll be out of here by tomorrow." Doctor Capaldi says, changing the topic and interfacing with the datapad by my bedside. "That's assuming that nobody's been daft about your nanites and got the readings wrong. We can come get you then."

"We also wanted to give you this." Leon says, handing me a small handmade doll. It had a mop of silver white hair and blue stitches across its face.

"Princess Lahani made it for you, and Princess Kelna helped." Leon adds, before sitting down at the foot of my hospital bed. "She insisted I give it to you the moment you woke up."

"You can thank them in person someday. Turns out we have a standing invitation to Faldan where the royal family is willing to sponsor us anything within reason." Bellona says.

"Thanks for coming to check on me." I say.

"It's always good to know you're well." Iñigo says.

"Yeah." Mick adds.

I beam. I swear I could take over the known galaxy with these guys.

Before I can pour my heart out about how lucky I am to have the best family this side of the known universe, the door opens again and a familiar voice cuts through the mood.

"Oh wow, am I interrupting anything?" Theron says. I can't see him, but it sounds like he's chewing.

Bellona squeals in genuine surprise.

"Just came here to deliver something." He adds.

I see him as the crew parts to let him through to my bedside. He's holding a box of cookies in one hand and a half-eaten cookie in the other. Bellona squeals again when she spots the box of cookies and begins clapping happily.

Theron sticks the half eaten cookie into his mouth, holding it between his teeth, and pulls out a datapad. He hands Iñigo the box before clicks a button on the pad. A muted holo springs up showing the crew of the Sol Pernix waving animatedly.

Almost as quickly as he brings it out, he clicks it off and hands the datapad to Doctor Capaldi, who accepts it with a scowl. Theron leans back, snaps up the cookie in his mouth without using his hands and begins to chew.

"Why don't you keep it safe for her while she's recovering, Doc?" Theron says, his mouth still full. He slows down his chewing as he realizes everyone is looking at him funny, except for Bellona, who still looks thrilled.

After a beat, recognition flashes through his eyes and he points to the box in Iñigo's hands. "Sorry, did you guys want some?"

Unbelievable.

He lets another beat pass before he slaps his forehead. "Riiight… no cookies… no actual digestive tract… or taste buds… got it. All good. Means more for me."

He smiles, takeing several cookies from the box with one hand and using the other one to grab one last cookie that he immediately bites into. "These are really good. You should totally get some. Deck Four. Look for Marcie. She sells 'em on the low to make a few credits on the side, no big. Totally worth it. Anyway, see ya."

With that, he walks out without even looking back.

The crew stands in complete silence, again with the exception of Bellona, who is keening at a very high frequency, all the while grinning like an idiot. She flutters on over to Iñigo, looks into the box and claps her hands rapidly before taking it. Immediately, she heads over to my bedside. On the way, she snags the datapad from Doctor Capaldi and hands me both items.

In a daze, I take both things from her and look into the box. There's still a full row of cookies left. From the look and smell of them, I recognize them immediately. And Bellona clearly had too, since she was there the first time we had both seen this kind of cookie.

It was on my third night on the Sol Pernix. We had finally escaped from Leghrelnis and were going to rendezvous with the Alliance. I had woken up from nightmares and found myself wandering aimlessly belowdecks until I bumped into Theron in the mess hall. I remember crying my eyes out to him before I realized Bellona was there too. I went over to hug her, and she did her best to reciprocate.

Theron leaned over to look me in the eye. He told me that there was nothing like a fresh batch of warm Mairinese Cookies to turn any bad thing into a good thing, and he made me a batch right then and there.

I scowl at the memory, and shake my head at the box. That liar. Marcie from Deck Four, my nanite enhanced ass.

Okay, I do not have the time, or the inclination, to unpack how dysfunctional it is that he can't just say things he feels out loud and thus has to resort to these vague coded gestures. Nor do I ever wish to validate this kind of behavior. I feel very strongly about that, especially now.

But I do, however, have the time to enjoy a handful of cookies with my crew as I play a message from some dear friends.

Bellona buzzes as I reach for a cookie and I almost end up throwing it at her face instead of taking a bite. It would be a waste of a good cookie, so I opt for the latter.

The girls are safe. With Faldan liberated, this war will turn in the Alliance's favor. Z is finally free from Conglomerate clutches. My family who are friends, and my friends who are family are all alive to fight another day.

I flick the switch on the datapad and unmute the holo to take in the well wishes from crew of the Pernix.

They go on for a few minutes. Tala jokes about how they should all just try their hand at play-acting for their performance with the Queen. Walsh jokes that they had to keep Dropshot quiet because he could not feign believable distress to save his life. Charles and Summer even managed to get Harlan and Pirsi to share their greetings.

Those two were a sight for sore eyes. Both of them were so excited that their jetpack mods worked wonders and saved such important lives. Which reminds me, I need to talk these two about that search and rescue upgrade idea I had earlier.

I shut the datapad off and take another bite, chewing slowly.

How long has it been since I'd felt this... content? Happy? I don't know what it is, really. All I know is that I have not felt this way since my first days on the Pernix.

So, why do I feel like there's something missing? Like there's a puzzle piece that hasn't quite clicked into place yet.

I glance at my crew. It's then that I spot Jean Philippe's 'facial expression', which to me was strikingly odd. And that's when it hits me. He smiles at the recognition in my eyes.

Jean Philippe's bonus target. Octavia's threat about the children of Leghrelnis. It all flashes before my eyes in a blur of color and heightened emotion.

JP comes close and pulls a datapad out of his pocket, and I audibly gasp.

"Is that what I think it is?" I ask. The cookie in my mouth turns to ash.

"It is." Jean Philippe says. "But also, it is so much more."

"Have you scanned these?" I ask. He shakes his head.

"We figured that if you were going to watch this, we should all watch it with you for the first time." Leon says.

"But you're sure it's in there. You found the right files on the Queen's closed network." I state.

The look on JP's face left little to the imagination. He was dead sure. I just wanted... no, *needed* to hear him say it.

"*Oui.*" He says simply. "I did ask Bellona to tell you I had a present for you."

With trembling hands, I reach for the datapad.

The first file is labeled Leghrelnis, Day Zero, Yuki Shirogane.

I skim the rest of the files. They are all labelled Leghrelnis, but they aren't just about me. They're about everything she did there. Everyone she's hurt there.

The children of Leghrelnis.

I steel myself as I open the first file. If I wanted to learn more about who I was, there was no better time than right now. And no better company to have by my side.

Bellona leans into me as I press play.

Here we go.

Transmission
Origin: Rosdthuige Black Site via subwarp back
channel 2X449Z.5

345dpwodnbo.aowfow013943huntsman.0.protocol.zavus.nandru.acti
vate.execute

Encrypted Counterresponse
Origin: Vector 559283

Full.data.shut.down.23043code7532w...

Rebooting...

Auxiliary.memory.wipe.routines.established...

...

...

Activated...

Awaiting orders . . .

ABOUT THE AUTHOR

Macky Santiago

A lot of Macky's childhood was spent making up stories and playing them out (with music and theatrics) for his little brother while said brother doodled and drew with the speed and tenacity that would foreshadow his (their?) future work ethic.

Today, that same energy has translated into the launching of BlueRoom Projects, the fulfillment of a life's worth of not-too-serious storytelling turned pretty serious storytelling.

When not holding story meetings with his brother Kahlil, Macky spends time with his lovely wife binge watching anime, reading books, vlogging about them on said wife's BookTube channel and eating lots and lots of food. Sometimes, he even cooks. Somewhere in between all of that is a podcast called FandomBuzzz and a TBR pile that just. won't. go. away.

ACKNOWLEDGMENTS

This first salvo would not have been possible if not for the following people:

My dad, who in so few words basically said I should write and find the time to do it. I love you.

My mom, who from day one said I should really do whatever I wanted in life. Who has not wavered once in supporting me. Thank you for always creating an atmosphere of creativity in my life. Would not have the confidence I have today to create had it not been for you. Vrepit Sa, mother. I love you always.

Nicole Gusto, for being the best copy-editing consultant this side of the known universe. Thank you for helping me keep accountable to the craft and for reading and editing earlier versions of this manuscript. I am eternally grateful for our opportunity to walk together as writers and dreamers of worlds. I will not be able to afford you if this keeps up.

Speaking of people I can't afford:

To Nazri Noor, for being so generous with your time and knowledge. And for always sharing your relevant experience as a writer. I have mentioned how you're like one of the fairy godmothers of this novella. Well, it's here and you're part of the process. Thank you! (Do grab his books if you love urban fantasy - start with the Darkling Mage series!)

To Michellan Sarile-Alagao, for always being open to reading my stuff long before I publish them. (Buy her poetry book! It's called After the Sunstone!)

To Micah Fernandez, who has been my mentor in storytelling. On and off, for years, you have been a source of wisdom and learning about the craft. You were generous with passing on what your mentors taught you, and you still are. Thank you for teaching me and partnering with me.

To my beta readers, thank you for the amazing feedback. This book would not be what it is without you. Special mention goes to New York friends (Steven) and family (Mel) who finished the book first and provided immediate feedback.

To Karen and Kevin Rama. You form some of the very core foundation of my life. I lean heavily on this foundation to function properly in this iteration of my life. I would quite literally be less of everything I am now without you. Love you both. Also, shoutout to Kev for being the tech side of this outfit and whipping that BlueRoom website into shape. Woohoo!

To Alexa Santiago, who forever suffers in the midst of all the unwritten and unfinished work she has been given the full behind-the-scenes tours of... Who lives languishing for the books I have yet to write *because* I have told her the beginnings, middles, and endings of some of them. Thank you for putting that extra shine and polish on this project. Thank you for believing in my work. You have no idea the amount of confidence you have given me to pursue this 'writer thing'. I love you always.

And finally, to Kahlil Santiago. brother, best friend and favorite artist of all time. Our friendship has grown (amazingly) into something that affords us this space where we can quite literally live the "PIXAR dream" of art inspiring story and story inspiring art. It has been one of my greatest joys bringing worlds to life with you. I am so glad we have both chosen to make this "the main thing" we do. Also, your art book is dope. People should check that out in the deluxe version. And if people do have the deluxe version right now, well... they get a chance to bask in the art that I love so much. Love you.

www.ingramcontent.com/pod-product-compliance
Lightning Source LLC
Chambersburg PA
CBHW022118170626
46808CB00002B/759